Diane Warner's
Complete Book of

Children's Parties

Make Birthdays and Every Other Children's Party a Fun Occasion

New Page Books
A Division of The Career Press, Inc.
Franklin Lakes, NJ

Diane Warner's Complete Book of Children's Parties
Cover design by Lu Rossman
Printed in the U.S.A. by Book-mart Press

To order this title, please call toll-free 1-800-CAREER-1 (NJ and Canada: 201-848-0310) to order using VISA or MasterCard, or for further information on books from Career Press.

The Career Press, Inc., 3 Tice Road, P.O. Box 687,
Franklin Lakes, NJ 07417
www.careerpress.com
www.newpagebooks.com

Library of Congress Cataloging-in-Publication Data

Warner, Diane.
    Diane Warner's complete book of children's parties : make birthdays and every other children's party a fun occasion / by Diane Warner.
        p. cm.
    Includes index.
    ISBN 1-56414-462-3 (pbk.)
    1. Children's parties. I. Title: Complete book of children's parties. II. Title.

GV1205 .W36 2000
793.2'1—dc21   00-056834

Dedication

To my beautiful little granddaughter, Lyndi Anne

Acknowledgments

I want to thank everyone who contributed to the success of this book, particularly my daughter, Lynn Paden, and my daughter-in-law, Lisa Warner, both of whom supplied me with helpful tips and refreshing original themes.

A special thanks to Gain von Fabrice, one of my *very* clever Tucson friends, who helped me with the title for the Super Sibling Selebration.

Thanks, too, to the Managing Editor at Career Press, Stacey A. Farkas, and the rest of the editorial staff there, who worked so hard on this book. And a very special thank you to John J. O'Sullivan, editor, who designed this book.

Contents

Introduction

This book is very much a result of the success of *Diane Warner's Big Book of Parties*. The party themes for children and teens described in *Big Book of Parties* spurred reader demand for even more creative themes, which resulted in an entire book devoted to this age group. It has been a joy gathering ideas and putting this book together for you!

As you will see, I cover all the basics of hosting a children's party, plus dozens of specific themes for everything from children's and teens' birthday parties to special occasion parties, seasonal parties, just-for-the-fun-of-it parties, party menus, recipes, and user-friendly planning sheets.

The title says it all—it is indeed the *complete* book of children's parties. If you can imagine it, you'll find it here.

Have fun and enjoy the planning!

Part 1

Party Basics

*P*lanning a children's party isn't rocket science, but there *are* a few basic things you need to know. For example, there are alternatives to the standard store-bought party invitations, new trends in theme decorating, and lots of popular games and activities that will make your party a success.

Read through this section first before choosing a theme for your party. You'll feel more confident about what is expected and how to go about it. Just remember—a child's party doesn't have to be perfect to be a success! Children are very forgiving—they just want to have a good time and won't even notice some little thing that happens to go wrong.

For stress-free planning, give yourself plenty of time—a month is ideal.

Chapter

1

Invitations

There are some cute fill-in-the-blanks invitations on the market, or you can create something original to go with your party's theme. I've included theme-oriented ideas throughout the book. For example, you can attach a hand-printed invitation to a black eye patch for a One-Eyed Pirate Party, or a dog biscuit for a Petting Zoo Party. In any case, you want your invitation to generate a sense of anticipation and excitement for your guests.

Here are other ways to customize an invitation:

☆ Create a customized invitation using a computer program, such as Broderbund's Print Shop Deluxe or Microsoft Publisher.

☆ Buy a coloring book and have your child color one page per guest. Then, remove the page from the coloring book, print the invitation across the top of the page and mail.

☆ Buy a book of paper dolls. Write the invitation on back of each paper doll and mail.

☆ Use your child's handprint to decorate the front of the invitation, the palm and each finger a different color of finger paint.

☆ Write out the invitation on blank post cards, using crayons or felt-tip markers. Send through the mail whole, or cut each post card into a jigsaw puzzle and send the pieces inside an envelope.

☆ Print the invitation on strips of paper approximately 4 by 2 in. Roll the strips into scrolls and insert them into balloons. Mail the deflated balloons in envelopes, along with instructions to blow up and pop the balloon to find the surprise inside.

☆ Gift wrap a sturdy piece of cardboard to resemble a present. Write the invitation on a small enclosure card and attach to the gift's ribbon.

These 10 things should be included on an invitation:

1. Name of the honored guest.
2. Name of the host(s).
3. Location of the party (with map or directions).
4. Date of the party.
5. Time of the party (be sure to include beginning and *ending* times).
6. Party's theme and dress code, if applicable.
7. What will be served (lunch, supper, cake).
8. Request for an R.S.V.P. (It's a good idea to include a deadline.)
9. Your telephone number.
10. Gift suggestions (if appropriate).

Tips

☆ Mail the invitations two or three weeks before the party.

☆ Always follow up a telephoned invitation with something in writing.

☆ It's usually not a good idea to have your child hand-carry written invitations to school to be handed out to those children who are invited. Not only can invitations become lost (by your child on the way to school, or by the invited guest on his way home), but there can be hurt feelings on the part of any children who are not invited.

☆ If the birthday child's sibling would rather not attend the party, that's fine. Especially if the sibling is older, he may prefer to spend time at a friend's house.

☆ A good rule of thumb: the number of guests should equal the child's age. For example, a 5-year-old would have five guests, and so on.

☆ Have a theme-oriented character hand deliver the invitations.

☆ A birthday party doesn't have to take place on the actual birthday itself. If the birthday falls during the week, it's common to schedule the party for the closest Saturday.

☆ The length of the party may range from an hour for a toddler to several hours for an older child. The average length of a grade-school-age birthday party is two hours.

Chapter

2

Decorations

Every party needs something in the way of decorations. You can get by with as little as a few colorful balloons, a tablecloth, plastic plates, and a festive cake. Or you can go all out with theme decorations, including everything from balloons at the front gate and luminaries along the front walk to tiki torches and floating rafts filled with fresh flowers for a teen's Hawaiian Luau.

Every party theme described in this book includes practical ways to customize decorations to complement your theme. However, if you only need a few easy, affordable ideas, here are the seven most popular ways to decorate for children's parties:

Balloons

Balloons are the biggest bang for the buck, not only because they're affordable, but because they give any party a festive feeling. As a matter of fact, even Winnie-the-Pooh says, "There is nobody that can be uncheered with a balloon." Balloon bouquets can be used as center-pieces, hung from a chandelier over the serving table, attached to chair backs or tied to the front gate. To cut down on cost, purchase your balloons in bulk from a party catalog or party supply store and rent or buy your own helium tank.

Tips:

    ✫   To blow up non-helium balloons, use a bicycle pump.

    ✫   Do *not* let the children blow up the balloons—a child can suffocate by inhaling them.

Paper Goods

Colorful paper tablecloth, plates, cups, napkins, and place cards are often all you need to "party-up" your table.

Tips:

    ✫   Use a white plastic tablecloth and write the children's names with a felt-tip marker at each place setting.

    ✫   Make a tablecloth by taping newspaper comic pages together.

    ✫   Use a colorful theme-oriented sheet as a tablecloth.

    ✫   Provide one solid-colored vinyl placemat per child. Let each child decorate his placemat with permanent felt-tip markers and stickers. (The place mats may be taken home as party favors.)

    ✫   In place of paper plates, serve the food in upside-down Frisbees. (The Frisbees may also double as party favors.)

    ✫   Place card alternatives:

        - Write each child's name on a helium balloon tied to the back of his chair.

        - Set one large sugar cookie at each place setting with the child's name written with frosting.

        - Place one goody bag at each place setting with the child's name written with felt-tip marker.

        - Write the children's names on tags attached to party favors that are set at each place setting.

Party Banners

You can purchase ready-to-use banners from your party supply store or you can generate personalized banners on your computer.

Crepe Paper or Holographic Streamers

Streamers will also splash color around the party site. For example, you can create a canopy over the serving table by suspending streamers from the ceiling and attaching them to the corners of the table.

Party Hats and Noisemakers

Provide guests with store-bought hats and noisemakers. Buy solid-colored party hats. Let each child decorate his own hat with stickers and felt-tip markers.

Party Favors

Colorful theme-oriented favors also add to the party's ambiance. They can be homemade or purchased. Favor suggestions are included in the party theme chapters that follow, but here are a few popular choices: kaleidoscopes, action figures, bubble blowers, kazoos, visors, yo-yos, sticker books, sunglasses, plastic cars, bracelets, gift certificates, jacks, telescopes, modeling clay, baseball cards, lollipops, mini-flashlights, jump ropes, marbles, paper dolls, plastic animals, pinwheels, necklaces, costume make-up, crayons, paint, or coloring books. For inexpensive toys and trinkets, order in bulk through one of the party catalogs listed in Resources, such as Oriental Trading Company, Birthday Express, U.S. Toy Company, or Benco Party Favors.

Favors can be distributed in several ways:

☆ Set them beside the place settings at the table.

☆ Place them in a basket to be handed out at the end of the party.

☆ Let them be "fished" for in one of two ways:

- Gift wrap the favors and tie them with large, loopy bows. Place them in a child's empty wading pool. Provide a "fishing pole" (a long stick with string and large opened metal paper clip as a hook). One at a time, let the children "fish" for their favors, hooking a bow with the fish hook.

- Tie a sheet between two trees or posts. Let the children fish for a favor by hanging the line over the sheet. One of your helpers stands on the other side of the sheet and "catches" a favor for each guest.

Goody Bags

Goody bags (also known as party bags, loot bags, or favor bags) are the trend these days for children's parties. Each child is given one to take home. It's filled with candies, favors, or small gifts, depending on the age of the guests. Younger children don't understand the concept of giving gifts (they want to receive them, not give them). So, while the birthday child is opening gifts, provide the guests with wrapped, inexpensive gifts of their own to open and take home in their goody bags. Goody bags can range from simple, decorated lunch bags to customized containers that match the party's theme, such as small painted buckets, burlap sacks tied at the neck with twine, or miniature pillowcases tied with ribbon. Keep your eyes open for anything that can be converted to a goody bag, such as popcorn cartons or painted cereal boxes (add ribbon handles), clear or colored cellophane sacks tied at the necks with ribbon, large drink cups with string handles, small baskets with handles, tulle pouches, painted egg cartons, and so on.

Decorate the bags using broad, felt-tip markers, wallpaper, fabric, or theme-oriented stickers, such as teddy bears for a Teddy Bear Party. *Note: Write the children's names on their bags, using a felt-tip marker or alphabet stickers.*

Tips:

- ✩ Here's a popular new idea: Let the children decorate for the party. All you need to do is set out crepe paper, balloons, streamers, favors, and table decorations, along with tape, scissors, and staplers.

- ✩ Dare to be creative! For example, decorate a synthetic Christmas tree with Valentine's cards and hearts for a Valentine's Party, or jack-o'-lanterns for Halloween, and so on. Or why not string colored Christmas lights around your patio for a summer party?

- ✩ If your party is being held after dark, you might want to create a magical ambiance by adding strings of tiny white lights and luminaries along your walkway. Luminaries are easy and inexpensive to make: Fill ordinary lunch sacks with three inches of sand and set a lighted votive candle inside each one. For a winter setting, create ice lanterns by freezing water in 36-ounce coffee cans, loosening the blocks of ice by running warm water over the coffee cans, chipping holes in the tops of the ice blocks, and inserting votive candles.

- ✩ Assemble a party box for your common party supplies. That way you'll have a head start on your next party. Fill the box with any leftover rolls of crepe paper, bags of balloons, name tags, place cards, party hats, streamers, candles, noisemakers, reusable luminaries, and so on, along with tape, scissors, and a stapler.

Chapter

3

Outdoor Games

ot all children's parties call for games, but if you'd like to include one or two, here are popular outdoor games for you to consider.

Miniature Golf

Create your own golf course on your lawn. Holes are created by laying paper cups on their sides and nailing them to the ground. Furnish standard golf clubs or putters, or use brooms or broom handles instead. You can use golf balls, small rubber balls or Ping-Pong balls. The child with the fewest number of strokes around the course is declared the winner.

Note: The competition can be a simple putting contest using a synthetic indoor putting green.

Fisherman's Net

Choose six children to serve as a "fisherman's net" that stands between two lines of contestants. The object is for the contestants on one side to escape to the other side without being caught in the fisherman's net. Each person who is caught in the net becomes part of the net and helps capture the next contestants who try to escape. As the game goes along, the fisherman's net becomes larger and larger until there is only one contestant who hasn't been caught in the net. This contestant is declared the winner.

Obstacle Course Relay Race

Enlist the help of your spouse or a friend to design an obstacle course in your backyard. The course should have a starting point and a finish line, with a dozen or so obstacles in between. Obstacles can include:

★   Old tires to hop in and out of.

★   A long plastic tube to squiggle through.

★   A wading pool to walk through barefoot (taking shoes on and off is part of the race).

★   A rope to jump rope with while hopping on one foot.

★   A large trash bag, stuffed with crushed newspapers, to jump over.

★   A croquet ball to knock through a hoop.

★   Monkey bars to swing across.

★   A Frisbee to balance on one's head while running a certain distance.

★   A narrow plank, about a foot off the ground, to walk across.

Divide the players into two or three teams. One team at a time sends a player through the course. As soon as the player has finished, he or she tags the next team member, who then traverses the course. Continue in this way until all the team members have participated. Record the time it takes for each team to run the course. The team with the shortest time wins.

Tennis Ball Baseball

Choose up two teams and play regulation baseball, except that instead of batting a baseball, the "batter" hits a pitched tennis ball with a tennis racket. Once the tennis ball has been hit, the game proceeds as in normal baseball, with players catching or throwing the tennis ball to the bases, and so on.

Beach Ball Baseball

This is similar to tennis ball baseball, except that the "batter" kicks a beach ball. There is no pitcher—the catcher places the ball on home plate for the batter to kick. Once the beach ball has been kicked, the game proceeds as in normal baseball.

Wheelbarrow Race

Ask your guests to pair off into groups of two. One member of each team walks on his hands while his partner holds onto his legs at the ankles. The pairs line up on the starting line, and at the signal, they race to the finish line. The winning pair receives a prize.

Tug of War

Choose two teams and place one group at each end of a rope about 100 feet long. Tie a bright ribbon at the middle of the rope. At a given signal, the teams begin to pull. The object is to pull the opposing team completely over to its side.

Shoelace Hop

Divide into teams of three. The children on each team stand side-by-side and connect their shoes with the shoes of the people on each side of them, using their shoelaces. (For those who aren't wearing laced shoes, provide ropes to tie their ankles together.) At the signal, the teams race to the finish line.

Flashlight Tag

This is a version of hide-and-seek that needs to be played in the dark. The children run and hide, and the person who's "it" looks for them with a flashlight. Each child who is "tagged" by the flashlight's beam is out. The game continues until the last child is found; that child becomes "it" for the next round.

Black Wolf

This is another version of hide-and-seek that also needs to be played in the dark. One child is the black wolf, and the rest of the children are the sheep. The object of the game is for the black wolf to sneak up on the sheep and, one at a time, drag the sheep back to its den. Once the sheep is in the wolf's den, however, he can escape if another sheep runs over and touches him before being caught by black wolf. Black wolf tries to stay hidden as much as possible so he can sneak up on the sheep, capture one and bring it to its den. The sheep hide from black wolf, but if they see black wolf sneaking up on them, they cry out, "black wolf—black wolf." The children take turns being black wolf.

Burlap Sack Race

Provide one burlap sack for each contestant. Stepping in and holding the sides of the sack with his hands, each contestant must run or jump to the finish line. (Falling down does not disqualify a contestant.) The contestant who reaches the finish line first is declared the winner.

Tip:

There are additional outdoor games included in the theme chapters that follow.

Chapter
4

Indoor Games

This chapter includes the most popular indoor children's party games. Some are rowdier than others, so you'll need to use your best judgment, depending on the space available and the age of your guests.

Pin the Tail on the Donkey

We all know how this game is played. You can purchase a Pin the Tail on the Donkey game, or you can create your own by drawing a donkey (or any other animal, such as a cow, cat, or pig) on a large piece of butcher paper and tacking it up on a wall. Blindfold the children one by one and ask them to pin (or tape) the tail on the animal. Another variation of this game is to tack up a dozen or so small inflated balloons and have the blindfolded children try to pop them with a pin.

Balloon Toss

This is a simple game for very young children. Gather the children in front of you, toss a balloon up in the air, and call out one of the children's names. That child tries to catch the balloon before it drops to the floor. If he succeeds, he gets to toss the balloon and call out another child's name.

Musical Clothes Bag

A few weeks before the party, begin assembling a trash bag full of silly clothes, boots, scarves, coats, hats, clown noses, novelty nightshirts, ski goggles, and so on. Arrange the children in a circle around the trash bag. Hand an apple to one of the children and have music begin to play. As the music plays, the children must pass the apple around the circle as fast as they can. When the music stops, the child caught holding the apple must go to the trash bag, close his eyes, pull something out and put it on. Start the music again and let the game continue until the trash bag is empty.

Penny Drop

Give each child 10 pennies. Have each child stand straight and try to drop the pennies, one by one, into a container sitting on the floor at his feet. Use an unbreakable container with a fairly narrow opening, such as a decorated soup can, a plastic cup, or a coffee can.

Barber Shop

Divide the guests into teams of two. Each team consists of one barber and one customer. Each barber is given a shaving mug filled with foamy soap, a brush and a "razor." (Use a rubber knife, tongue depressor or a child's toy razor.) When you say "Go," each barber ties an apron around the neck of his customer, lathers up his face and gives him a "shave." The judge watches each team to be sure each customer's face is thoroughly lathered and "shaved" without allowing lather to drop onto the floor or the apron. The barber who has shaved his customer the best in the least time wins.

Simon Says

Simon Says is a game where one leader (Simon) stands in front of a line of contestants and tells them what to do, prefacing each command with "Simon says...." For example, the leader may say, "Simon says, touch your nose," or "Simon says, stick out your tongue." Then (this is the tricky part), the leader slips in a quik command *not* prefaced by the words "Simon says." Every child who follows a command not prefaced with "Simon says...," is out of th e game.

Shoe Basket

Ask the children to remove their shoes and dump them into a large laundry basket. When you say "Go," all of the children run to the basket to find their shoes and put them on. The first child to tie the laces or buckle the straps on both shoes is the winner. (For children under age 5, it isn't necessary to lace or buckle the shoes.)

Mummy Wrap

Divide the group into two teams. One member of each team volunteers to be the mummy. Furnish each team with a large roll of toilet paper and a roll of tape. When you say "Go," team members begin to wrap their mummies in toilet paper, leaving small peep holes for the eyes. (If a piece of toilet paper breaks off, they must tape it back together.) The first team to use up the roll of toilet paper wins.

Sweat Suit Stuff

Divide the guests into two teams. Ask each team to choose their shortest member to wear extra large sweatpants and an extra large sweatshirt over his clothes. Furnish each team with 40 small, inflated balloons. At the signal, see which team can stuff the most balloons inside the sweat suit without breaking them. Call time at the end of two minutes.

Orange-Under-the-Chin Race

Divide the guests into two teams. Ask each team to line up in a straight line. Give one orange to each team leader. The goal is to see which team can pass the orange, chin to chin, down the line the fastest without dropping it. If a team member drops the orange, the team must start over.

Musical Chairs

Place one chair per child in a circle, with the seats facing out. Have the children stand in front of their respective chairs; play music and have them march around the circle. While the music is playing, remove one chair. When the music stops, the children scramble to find a chair to sit in. Of course, one child will be eliminated each round until there are only two contestants and one chair left. The child who lands in that last chair is declared the winner. To prevent any hard feelings among younger children, it's nice to present each child with a small wrapped gift as he is eliminated from the game. Another way to prevent hard feelings is to have an equal number of chairs as there are participants. One of the chairs is designated "king of the hill." That way, every time the music stops, one child gets to be in the special chair.

Untie the Knots

Choose one child to be "it." That child leaves the room while the remaining children join hands in a circle and tie themselves in "knots" by ducking under, stepping over, and winding around each other, without letting go of each others' hands. The child who is "it" is called back into the room and must untie the knots without undoing the clasped hands. This is accomplished by instructing children. For example, the child who is "it" may say, "Becky, step over this knot." (Each "knot" consists of two clasped hands.)

String Pass

Divide the children into teams of four or five each. Provide each team with a long string with large safety pins attached to each end. When you say "Go," the child at the head of each line attaches one of the safety pins to his shirt, then passes the other pin down through his shorts or pants. The next person in line must bring the pin up through his clothing, and so forth. The first team to pass the string to the end of the line with the last pin fastened wins.

Mystery Socks

Fill a dozen or so socks with a variety of items that have identifiable shapes, such as a clothespin, fork, yo-yo, etc. Provide each child with a piece of paper and a pencil, then arrange the children in a circle. Ask the children to identify the items by feeling them through the socks and to write down what they think they are. When each child has had a turn to feel all the socks and write down his guesses, empty the socks onto the floor. The child with the most correct answers wins.

Ping-Pong Ball Hunt

Upon arrival, give each guest a Ping-Pong ball with his or her name on it. Ask him to hide the ball very well anywhere in the house (or the yard, or within a certain room). When the last guest has arrived and hidden a ball, send all the children on a hunt for the balls. The winner is the child whose ball is the last to be found.

Spoon Race

Divide the group into teams and arrange the teams in lines. Furnish each player with a teaspoon and each team with one item to be passed from spoon to spoon, such as a cotton ball, Ping-Pong ball, olive, grape, or a piece of popcorn. The team leader, who is at the head of the line, passes the object from his or her spoon to the spoon of the next team member in line, and so on down the line. Every time the object is dropped, the team must start over. The first team to pass the object from beginning to end without dropping it is declared the winner. Some variations on this game include:

Raw Egg Race

This game is played outdoors, with a raw egg as the object on the spoon.

Tennis Ball Race

Players pass a tennis ball using only their elbows.

Straw and Ball Race

Players compete to be the first to get a Ping-Pong ball across the room or lawn by blowing on it through a drinking straw.

Balloon Race

Players pass a balloon using only their knees.

Lemon Race

This is a variation of the Straw and Ball Race; players roll a lemon across the floor or lawn using the eraser end of a pencil.

Kiddie Limbo

Have two adults hold the ends of a six-foot dowel or broom- stick three feet off the ground. As festive music plays, the children lean backward as they dance under the dowel or broomstick. If they touch the stick or ground with any part of their body, they are disqualified. After all the children have successfully limboed under the stick, the stick is lowered and the children give it another try. The stick continues to be lowered until only one child is able to get under the stick without falling or touching the stick or the ground.

Musical Statues

Assemble the children in a circle. Whenever the music plays, the children are to dance around the circle, freezing in place whenever the music stops. Don't start the music again until someone moves (even blinking or smiling counts). Believe me, it won't take long! Whoever moves is out of the game. Continue until only one child is left and declared the winner.

Try to Remember

Place several items on a tray, such as a can of dog food, hairbrush, spoon, baseball, action figure, etc. The older the children, the more items on the tray. Ask the children to look at the items and try to remember them. Then remove the tray from the room. Have the children write down the items from memory. The child with the most correct answers is the winner.

Telephone

Arrange the children in a circle. Begin the game by whispering a sentence into the ear of the first person in the circle, such as, "The little boy went to the store to buy a green yo-yo for his Grandpa." The first person whispers the sentence to the next person, and so forth, until finally the last person says it out loud. The fun of the game is that the final version be different from the original. For example, "We went to the beach this summer and I found a big sea shell" could become, "We went to a bridge this summer with a pig named Michelle." Once the children get the hang of the game, they can make up their own sentences to whisper to each other.

Tip:

Additional indoor games can be found in the theme chapters that follow.

Chapter
5

Crafts and Activities

*I*n addition to games, there are also party crafts and other activities that are appropriate, depending on the age of the guests and the party's theme. This chapter offers a variety of crafts and activities to consider.

Crafts

Decorated Mural

Purchase a long piece of butcher paper from a teachers' supply store. Attach it horizontally along a wall and assign each guest a section to decorate. Be sure each child "signs" or initials his or her section so it can be cut out and brought home as a souvenir of the party. If your party has a theme, such as a Mother Goose party, ask the guests to draw appropriate characters. Optional: Have the children sit at a table and decorate a white plastic tablecloth.

Self-Portraits

Cut butcher paper into child-size lengths. Have each child lie down on a piece of paper and let another child outline his body with pencil. (Be sure the child's fingers are spread apart so each finger can be traced.) Each child colors in his own features, including face, hair, clothes, etc. You can furnish large crayons or tempera paint. The children take their self-portraits home as party souvenirs.

Sidewalk Art

Provide washable sidewalk chalk for the children to use as they draw pictures on the sidewalk. (This is a good filler activity while waiting for the rest of the guests to arrive.)

Coloring Books and Crayons

Give the guests their own coloring books and small boxes of crayons as they arrive for the party. Provide a table where they can sit down and color quietly as the rest of the guests arrive.

Play Dough

This is a great end-of-the-party activity, something to entertain the children as the parents are arriving to pick them up. Supply each child with his own plastic bag of homemade play dough. Seat the children around a table that has been covered with a plastic disposable tablecloth. The children can amuse themselves by forming their dough into various shapes.

Here is an eight-child recipe:

☆   2 cups white flour.
☆   1 cup salt.
☆   4 tablespoons vegetable oil.
☆   1 drop food coloring.
☆   Water as needed.

Mix all the ingredients together. Add water, a drop at a time, until the dough is workable. (You can adapt this recipe for a larger number of children.)

String-a-Necklace Contest

Provide bowls of miniature marshmallows, Cheerios, Life Savers, popcorn, miniature pretzels, gum drops, licorice, or any other foods that can be threaded onto a string. Give each child a long piece of string, pre-threaded onto a large, blunt needle. Tell the children to begin threading their necklaces when you say "Go." Set a timer for three minutes. When the timer rings, the child with the most items on his or her string wins. Of course, the children may keep their necklaces as edible party favors.

T-Shirt Art

Purchase three-packs of men's white size small T-shirts. Cut cardboard "torsos" to fit snugly inside the T-shirts (to prevent the paint from bleeding through from front to back, and to stretch the fabric taut for painting.) Provide fabric paints and brushes, as well as stencils and sponge stamps that go with the party's theme.

Create a Box City

We've all heard that children would rather play with the box than the toy inside, and it certainly is true in this case. Before the party, collect an assortment of large cardboard boxes (preferably from your local appliance store). Set them in a row in your party room or on your patio, creating a miniature street. Provide the children with felt-tip markers and an assortment of crayons, and let them design a "city," with one box as the grocery store, another as the barber shop, another as the gas station, some as houses, and so on. Or, depending on your party's theme, they can turn the boxes into space ships, pirate ships, prehistoric caves, or doll houses.

Glove Puppets

Purchase inexpensive cotton gardening gloves—you'll need one glove per child. Let the children turn the fingers into puppets by drawing faces with pens and felt-tip markers, gluing on strips of yarn hair, and making collars and ties by tying ribbons around their "necks."

Activities

Children's Sing-Along

Younger children enjoy singing traditional pre-school and primary-age songs, such as "Itsy Bitsy Spider," "The Farmer in the Dell," "Ring Around the Rosie," and "Mary Had a Little Lamb." If you aren't familiar with these songs, you can pick up a sing-along tape from a bookstore, music store, or teachers' supply store. You can also find them on an audiocassette tape called Sing-Along Birthday Songs. (See Resources.)

Story Time

There is nothing like a good story to fill five or 10 minutes of party time for the younger set. The best stories are those with big, bright pictures, and plenty of action or mystery, or with a little acting required on your part, as you play the part of the big mean lion or the pretty princess. Practice reading and acting out the story ahead of time, giving thought to props you might use.

Kazoo Marching Band

Provide kazoos for the children to play as they parade around the house, the yard or—if you dare—around the block. Let the adults play other instruments, such as oatmeal box drums, sand paper blocks or rhythm sticks. Choose a melody the children already know, such as "Twinkle, Twinkle, Little Star" or "Mary Had a Little Lamb." (Not that anyone will actually recognize the melody as they march along.)

Piñatas

A piñata is a papier-mâché animal or figure that is elaborately decorated and filled with candy or small toys. The piñata is suspended by a rope or pulley from a tree branch or a hook overhead. The children are blindfolded, one at a time, and told to swing at the piñata with a broom. An adult controls the location of the piñata by raising or lowering the rope. Each child has three swings, hoping to break the piñata so he can retrieve the goodies inside. By controlling the piñata's location, the adult can prevent it from being broken until hit by the last contestant. Once broken, the children rush to gather up the candies or toys. To prevent hurt feelings, have an additional supply of goodies on hand that can be used to even out the distribution.

To make a piñata easily and inexpensively:

Fill a large paper grocery bag with toys and candies. Paint the bag with tempera paint and decorate by stapling crepe paper streamers to the bottom and sides. Tie the bag closed at the top with a brightly colored cord and suspend from a branch or hook.

Opening of Gifts

The opening of gifts can have its problems, especially for young children who may have built up such high expectations regarding their gifts that they are disappointed. Or, the child may receive duplicates or triplicates of the same gift. This can be a huge letdown and may even result in tears or a temper tantrum. Another problem can be the reluctance of a guest to part with the gift he or she has brought to the party. In fact, the child may actually have to be coaxed to give it up. A solution to the first problem is to plan the opening of gifts as the last activity of the party. That way, if the birthday girl or boy is less than enthused about the gifts, there will be less time to show it. Days before the party, the child should also be coached on how to act courteously when it's time to open gifts at the party. The second problem has an easier solution. In order to ease the pain of relinquishing a gift, load the child up with lots of gifts of his or her own to take home, such as prizes, a party hat, and a party bag containing favors, small games and toys, and candy.

Awarding of Door Prizes

Here are two creative ways to award door prizes:

1. Number and wad up tiny pieces of paper, one per prize. Insert them inside three balloons *before* the balloons are blown up with helium gas. Arrange the balloons in a bouquet as part of the decorations. Then, near the end of the party, ask the guest of honor to choose one of the balloons and burst it by sitting on it (no hands allowed!) The wad of paper is then unfolded and the number read. The person with the corresponding number on the bottom of his paper cup or plate wins a door prize. Repeat until all door prizes have been awarded.

2. Give one blown-up balloon to each child. Each balloon has a number inside that corresponds to a gift displayed on a table. The child sits on his or her balloon until it pops, then takes his number to the table and takes the corresponding gift, which becomes his or her "door prize" or party favor. This is a good idea for a young child's birthday party because a guest in this age bracket sometimes feels sad when he doesn't have a gift to open.

Chapter

6

Games and Activities for Teens

Teens are easier to entertain than small children. All a teen party really needs is the teens' music played over a good sound system and plenty of food.

However, if you are looking for a few games and activities to fill the time, here are some popular ideas:

Who Am I?

This is a great get-acquainted game because it forces the guests to talk to each other. Purchase a supply of 3 x 5 cards and write the name of a famous person on each. Pin one of these cards to each player's back. Each person can see the names on the backs of the other guests, but can't, of course, see his own. The idea of the game is for a player to determine whose name is pinned on his back by asking questions about that person. As the game begins, each player is allowed to ask three questions per round that can be answered only with a "yes" or "no." Such as, "Am I living?" "Am I a female?" "Am I an American?" The first player to guess the name on his back wins a prize. By the way, be sure to have a few extra prizes on hand, in case of a tie.

Mystery Guest Game

The kids are given a list of five questions they are to ask as many guests as possible in 20 minutes, recording the answers as they go along. When the 20 minutes are up, the host secretly chooses one guest as the mystery guest. He then describes the mystery guest and the first person who knows the mystery guest's identity wins. The idea of this game, of course, is to help the guests get acquainted with each other. You can come up with your own list of questions, but here are examples:

★   What is your favorite sport?

★   How many brothers and sisters do you have?

★   What is your favorite food?

Charades

Charades is probably the most popular party game in America today. Divide the kids into two teams. Each team comes up with the titles of six or eight books, movies, television shows or songs. They write the titles on pieces of paper which are folded up and placed in a basket. The teams take turns drawing a piece of paper from the opposing team's basket, although the only person who sees the title is the person who'll be acting it out. A timer is set and this person has three minutes to silently act out the title, using his hands, body and facial expressions to communicate the title to his team. If the timer "rings" before the team has guessed the title, the opposing team gets five points. If the team guesses the title before the timer "rings," they get ten points. After each side has had six or eight turns, the team with the most points wins. In the case of a tie, play one more round.

Variation 1

A clever way to furnish the titles is to write them on small pieces of paper and insert them inside deflated balloons, along with a little confetti. Fill them with helium, tie them with long strings, and let the balloons float to the ceiling. Then, instead of drawing a wad of paper from a basket, the contestant selects a balloon, pops it, and retrieves the piece of paper that states the title.

Variation 2

Another version of this game is to draw the clues instead of acting them out, resulting in a game very similar to Pictionary.

Note: Not everyone is comfortable acting out in front of a group, so it's a good idea to have fewer turns per side than there are team members. This allows any team member to decline graciously without feeling pressured.

Identify the Sounds

A week or so before the party, record 20 or 30 sounds on a cassette tape. Verbally identify each sound with a number before recording the sound. For example, say, "Sound number one" before recording an alarm clock ringing, etc. During the party, give the kids paper and pencil and ask them to identify each sound as it is played. The player who identifies the most sounds correctly is the winner. Suggested sounds to record: toilet flushing, car horn honking, cat meowing, coffee pot brewing, washer on spin cycle, leaf blower, dog barking, thunder, electric toothbrush, bird chirping, garage door opening, clarinet playing, baby doll crying, and so on.

Dictionary Game

Assemble a dictionary, several pads of note paper, and pens. The idea of this game is to choose an unusual word from the dictionary that is unfamiliar to the players.

Round One:

* ☆ **Step 1**—A person is chosen to be the leader of round one; he announces the word he has chosen to the group. If anyone knows the meaning of the word, the word is disqualified and another must be selected.

* ☆ **Step 2**—The leader writes the true dictionary definition of the word on a piece of paper.

* ☆ **Step 3**—The remaining players write down fictional definitions that are as believable as possible.

* ☆ **Step 4**—All pieces of paper are turned in to the leader, who reads each definition out loud, maintaining as straight a face as possible.

* ☆ **Step 5**—Each player announces which definition he believes to be true.

* ☆ **Step 6**—Each player who has chosen the correct definition receives one point. Each player whose false definition was chosen by another player receives one point. The leader receives five points if no one chose the correct dictionary definition.

This is the end of round one. Play continues as another player is chosen to be the leader, and so on until everyone has had a turn. The winner is the player with the most total points at the end of all the rounds.

Clothespin Game

Purchase a supply of colorful plastic clothespins. Pin one clothespin on each guest's clothing and let the game begin. Set a timer for 20 minutes. During that 20-minute period no one is allowed to say the word "no." So, the idea of the game is to ask the guests questions about themselves, baiting them to answer with a "no." Any guest who does must relinquish his clothespin to the person who tricked him into saying the forbidden word. When the timer rings, the guest with the most clothespins wins.

Observation Game

Arrange 15 or 20 items on a tray, such as a pocket knife, a pencil, a fork, and so forth. Then ask a friend or your co-host to walk slowly around the room, displaying the tray for all the guests to see. Everyone is given paper and pencil, and as soon as your friend has left the room with the tray, the guests will be asked to write down as many things as they can remember about your friend! (Color of hair and eyes, what she was wearing, and so on.) The kids will moan and complain, of course, but they'll finally settle down and start recording things they remember about your friend. The guest who has recorded the most accurate description wins a prize.

Karaoke

Rent a karaoke machine (see Disc Jockeys in your Yellow Pages) and you'll have all the entertainment you can handle, especially for the teen crowd. Usually one or two will have sung to a karaoke machine before, and with just a little encouragement, they'll be glad to demonstrate how the concept works. The next thing you know, they're really enjoying themselves, which will encourage the rest of the kids to give it a try.

Frisbee Golf

Create a golf course (in your yard or in a field or park) by designating certain natural or man-made markers as the greens. The object is to see who can get from tee to green on each hole in the least number of Frisbee throws. Use golf cards to keep score, or create your own on 3 x 5 cards.

Tip

See additional games, races, and activities in Chapter 67 (Carnivals), Chapter 68 (Indoor Olympics) and Chapter 69 (Field Day).

Chapter
7

Entertainment

The current trend is toward providing specialty entertainment for children's parties. Here are some popular choices.

Jump Delight Party Playground

Jump Delights, also known as Theme Party Jumps and Dino Jumps, can be rented for your party. (Look under Party Supplies or Party Rentals in your Yellow Pages.) These inflatable jumps are delivered to your party site by the rental companies, and they are available in various sizes and themes. For example, there are Barney Jumps, Lion Jumps, Dino Dens, and Power Dens. The rental costs run from about $50 for a two-hour rental to about $115 for four hours. This usually includes delivery and pickup.

Face Painting

Children love to have their faces painted. Hire a professional to entertain at your party by creating clown faces, or purchase face paints and do it yourself.

Balloon Artist

Have a balloon artist entertain the children by creating balloon animals, hats, and other shapes.

Magician

Hire a magician to entertain the children with his sleight of hand.

Clown

A clown is a tried-and-true choice for a children's party.

Caricaturist

Let the kids take their caricatures home as party favors.

Pony Rides

Pony rides are also a hit, especially with the younger children.

Petting Zoo

Some areas of the country have traveling petting zoos available for children's parties.

Tips

Most of the children's party entertainers mentioned above perform part-time, so the best way to locate one of these artists is by word-of-mouth. Ask friends, teachers, and other parents for references, or you may find some listed in the yellow pages. Look under "Party Suppliers," "Clowns," "Artists," "Pony Rentals," "Magicians," "Entertainers," and "Entertainment Agencies." These entertainers usually charge a flat rate or by the hour, their fees varying widely throughout the country. However, you can expect to pay in the neighborhood of $100 to $150 total.

Always have a children's video on hand—just in case you need a filler at the end of the party while you wait for parents to pick up their children.

Chapter

8

Need a Little Help?

Don't be afraid to ask for a little help if you need it. A friend may agree to co-host the party with you, or perhaps a few teenagers can help you out, especially during a party for the younger set.

These are the areas where help is usually appreciated:

1. Addressing invitations.
2. Hosting a birthday party for a baby or young child (invite one parent or helper per guest).
3. Hosting a party for an older child (you will need one adult per six to eight guests).
4. Hosting a teen party with more than 12 guests.
5. Making decorations, favors, name tags, place cards.
6. Preparing and serving the party food.
7. Helping with the party games and activities.

Tip

If it will be a large party with a mixture of children and adults, why not give some consideration to having it catered? Let the caterer worry about buying the food, preparing it, serving it, and cleaning up the mess! The added expense may not be as much as you would expect, and it will allow you to relax and enjoy the party from beginning to end!

Part 2

Birthday Parties for Children

*T*his section will give you easy, creative ideas for planning your child's birthday party. It begins with a chapter about birthday expectations according to age group, and is followed by destination party ideas and several chapters filled with children's birthday party themes. You'll see that I have given each party theme a suggested age level, but you know your child's likes and dislikes better than I do, so don't be afraid to choose a party theme from a different age category. The important thing to remember is that this is not *your* party—it is your *child's* party, so be sure to talk things over and let him or her decide what sounds like the most fun!

Chapter
9

Birthday Expectations by Age Group

As you consider the party themes in the following chapters, you'll notice they are arranged by age groups. There is no such thing as a one-size-fits-all party theme, so it's important to know what type of party is suitable for each age.

Here are a few general rules that may be helpful as you consider the various party theme possibilities.

Age 1

A baby has absolutely no expectations when it comes to celebrating his or her first birthday. The expectations come from parents, grandparents, and other friends and relatives.

Age 2

By age 2 a child is actually able to grasp the concept of a party and is quite excited by it. Although the 2-year-old really gets into the fun of the party with the birthday hats, blowing out the candles on the cake and the opening of gifts, he is still a baby in many ways. Don't expect too much from this tiny host, because he will tend to tire easily and want his Mommy or Daddy to stay close by his side.

Age 3

By age 3 a child has finally reached a stage where she truly understands the concept of a party. For one thing, she has probably attended several and realizes that a party provides fun and gifts and games. One problem that often arises at one of these parties, unfortunately, is squabbling among the children. However, with plenty of adult supervision, squabbling children can be tactfully separated from one another and the party can continue with little damage.

Age 4

A 4-year-old is not only enthusiastic beyond belief, but totally cooperative with the planned activities. Children in this age group usually interact well during a party and, in fact, will go, go, go until they drop.

Age 5

Oh, if only the 5-year-olds could be as amiable as the 4-year olds. But, alas, children in this age group sometimes enter a period of self-consciousness where it takes a little more effort to coax them into participating in planned activities. Another problem with 5-year-olds is that they become very possessive of any prizes or favors they may acquire during the party and, if they misplace theirs momentarily, may snatch them away from one of the other guests. A solution for this little problem is to plan ahead by providing each child with his own personalized goody bag to keep track of his newly acquired treasures.

Age 6

A 6-year-old likes to get involved in the planning of her party and, in fact, will probably have a definite party theme in mind. Children in this age group are extremely competitive, so you'll need plenty of take-home goodies, including duplicate prizes for any games that are played.

Age 7

A 7-year-old birthday child also wants to be involved in the planning of his party and usually works well with the adult who is making the party decisions. The party itself, however, can become a little wild, due to the exuberance of children in this age group. Be sure to have plenty of adults on hand to help control the energy level.

Age 8

Ah, the 8-year old! You'll notice quite a change in your child from his last birthday to this one because he has become less tolerant of a lot of things—including the opposite sex. Which is why a boy/girl party doesn't usually work as well as a same-sex party. Also, 8-year-olds' attention spans seem to revert to those of a 2-year-old, which is why you may decide to have a destination party, where the children will stay entertained.

Age 9

Although a 9-year-old may not put it exactly this way, his thinking is that of someone who's "been there, done that." It takes a lot to impress a 9-year-old! Choose a theme for his party that he's never even heard of before! Keep the party moving and add several competitive-type games, such as relays or tugs-of-war. Note of caution: keep mixing up the teams so that no one child will feel he has caused his team to lose an event. Good luck—9-year-olds are a challenge!

Age 10

I love the 10-year old! He's enthusiastic, responsive to ideas, eager to help out, and appreciative of your efforts and party preparations. This will be one of the easiest parties you'll ever host.

Age 11

By age 11, the boy-girl problem has again developed, which can make party-planning a little stressful. For example, the birthday girl may want to invite boys to her party. However, boys won't want to attend, and if they do, you may find they become insulting or obnoxious toward the girls. The birthday boy, on the other hand, wouldn't think of inviting girls to his party, and whatever you do, don't encourage it, or you may be sorry.

An all-girl party has its own little problems as well, because 11-year-old girls are at the stage where they tend to form cliques and rivalries. My personal advice is to plan an all-boy or all-girl party at this age and keep them so busy with fun activities that there is no time for friction to develop.

You may want to consider a destination for the party where there is a high level of activity, such as a bowling alley, amusement park, or family fun center where the children can run around from one game to the other.

Age 12

By the time a child has reached the age of 12, you're looking at a less structured, more sophisticated birthday party, such as a slumber party, scavenger hunt or a San Francisco Party (see Chapter 38). Fortunately, by this age (what a difference a year makes), boys and girls are getting along with each other a little better than before and you may want to plan a boy/girl party.

Chapter

10

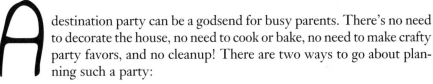

Destination Parties for Kids

A destination party can be a godsend for busy parents. There's no need to decorate the house, no need to cook or bake, no need to make crafty party favors, and no cleanup! There are two ways to go about planning such a party:

1. A visit to a fun site, such as a fast-food restaurant, the zoo, a children's movie, a hands-on museum, the local fire department, an amusement park, a laser game center, an ice-cream parlor, a chartered boat, a video arcade, a sight-seeing train, a nature center, an aquarium, a mini-golf course, or skating rink, followed by a mini-party at your house with cake and gifts.

2. A special birthday party package offered by any of the afore-mentioned venues.

The following are examples of party packages offered by two national establishments. (Costs vary with location.)

⭐ McDonald's restaurants: A $30 option includes a sundae and orange soda for 10 children, party favors, a birthday cake, party games, a photo of the birthday child, and a group photo. A $45 option includes a meal for 10 children, party favors, a birthday cake, party games, a birthday child photo, and a group photo.

⭐ Chuck E. Cheese's restaurants: $9.99 per child (for a minimum of six and a maximum of 30) includes pizza, beverages, birthday cake, $4 in tokens per child, a decorated table, a live show with Chuck E. Cheese, and the services of a birthday hostess.

Tips

⭐ Plan your own destination for a party. For example, if you have a train station near your home, buy tickets for the children to ride for thirty minutes or so, get off the train, treat the children to ice cream cones at the local Baskin-Robbins, then get back on the train for the trip back home.

⭐ Or, how about taking the kids fishing (with real poles and real fish), hiking, or swimming at the beach? Kids also love airports, sightseeing boats or ferries, and farms. Pretend you're a teacher and you're planning a field trip—it may turn out to be the best destination party your child has ever had!

Chapter

11

Balloon Party (Age 1)

A birthday party for a one-year old can't fail—at least from the baby's perspective— because he has no expectations whatsoever. That's not to say he won't cry because he's fussy, or because he needs a nap, but I guarantee he won't cry because the party was a flop! The only expectations come from parents, grandparents, and other relatives, and if they're expecting a theme party, you can borrow from some of the other ideas in this section. For example, you can host a Teddy Bear Party (Chapter 13) or adopt a Mother Goose character as your theme (Chapter 12).

However, if your main goal is to please your baby, all you need to do is splash around a lot of color—babies love bright colors—and what better way than with dozens of balloons. Let balloons be your theme, for everything from the invitations to the decorations to the birthday cake.

Invitations

☆ Blow up one large balloon for each invitation and use a permanent felt-tip marker to print the invitation on each balloon. Deflate the balloons, insert in envelopes and mail.

Attire

☆ Ask the guests to come dressed in bright colors.

Decorations

☆ Bright helium balloons, of course! Tie them to the backs of chairs, arrange in bouquets on the table and around the room, and attach a cluster to the front gate or entryway. Cover the ceiling with balloons (to be used later in the party). Be sure there are several tied to the back of birthday baby's high chair—photo-ops, you know!

☆ Colorful birthday hats are a must, of course.

☆ Decorate the birthday cake with colorful frosting balloons—set the cake in the center of the table.

☆ Suspend colorful strands of crepe paper and crinkle-tie ribbons from the ceiling over the table.

Amusements

☆ Hire a balloon artist to make balloon animals for the children.

☆ Play balloon volleyball by bopping a balloon back and forth over a table or chair (this should not be a helium-filled balloon).

☆ Each guest grabs several helium balloons from the ceiling of the party site, takes them outside, and lets them go. The babies will love watching the colored balloons lift up into the sky.

☆ Take Polaroid instant photos of each guest and send them home as party favors. Take plenty of extras for your baby's memory book.

☆ Videotape all the festivities and show the tape near the end of the party.

Edibles

☆ Serve baby finger foods, such as round balloon peanut butter and jelly sandwiches and round balloon cookies (frost with red and blue frosting and add strings cut from licorice vines.)

☆ Birthday cake and ice cream are the highlights of this party, so light that candle and take photos galore! For a special touch, add sparklers to the cake and light before setting the cake in front of the baby—another memorable photo for baby's book.

Prizes and favors

☆ Balloons, small toys, balloon animals, instant photos.

Tips

☆ Be prepared to comfort the children if any balloons pop during the party.

☆ If a balloon should happen to pop or deflate, gather up the pieces and throw them away immediately—don't let the babies touch them or put them in their mouths.

☆ Be flexible! If the birthday boy falls asleep during the party—that's okay! Or, if he throws his beautiful balloon cookie and sandwich on the floor—what difference does it really make? Absolutely none!

Chapter

12

Mother Goose Party (Ages 2-6)

This is a versatile theme because you can plan your party around any one or more of your child's favorite Mother Goose characters, including Humpty Dumpty, the Three Little Pigs, Little Miss Muffett, Little Bo-Peep, and so forth.

Invitations

☆   There are dozens of Mother Goose theme invitations available on the market, or you can create your own, depending on the characters you have chosen. For example, if you choose a Three Bears theme, you can send tiny teddy bears with invitations attached to their wrists.

Attire

☆   Greet the children at the door dressed as a Mother Goose character, such as Little Red Riding Hood.

Decorations

☆   Move one of your silk house plants or silk trees into your party room and decorate it with tiny white lights, ribbons, and gumballs (use a large-holed needle and yarn to thread through the gumballs in order to hang them).

☆ Purchase a dozen or so helium balloons, several with Mother Goose characters on them. Tie them to the backs of chairs or place them in clusters around the room.

☆ Create a table centerpiece based on your theme. For example, if your theme is the nursery rhyme "Little Miss Muffett," set a doll on a pillow beneath a giant spider suspended from the ceiling over her head. For "Mary Had a Little Lamb," use a doll with her arm around a stuffed lamb.

Amusements

☆ Kazoo Marching Band—The children can march to a recorded nursery rhyme, such as "Mary Had a Little Lamb." The younger children may not be familiar with kazoos, but they will catch on fast. Of course, the kazoos may be taken home as party favors.

☆ Humpty Dumpty Says—like Simon Says.

☆ Story Time—Read several Mother Goose stories and ask the children to act out the characters in the story. For example, "The Three Little Pigs" will need a cast consisting of three pigs and a wolf.

☆ Show the *Cinderella* video or another favorite.

Edibles

☆ Magic Wand Snacks—straight pretzels or red cocktail straws dipped in peanut butter.

☆ Little Boy Blue's Favorite Treat—macaroni and cheese, served with hot dogs dipped in catsup.

☆ Decorated birthday cake depicting the party's theme—a cow jumping over the moon, Humpty Dumpty sitting on a wall, and so on.

☆ Goldilocks' Sundaes—Scoops of ice cream with yellow candy sprinkles on top.

Prizes and favors

☆ Coloring books, story books, face paints, tiny stuffed animals.

Tip

☆ This party can also be adapted to a Disney or *Sesame Street* character.

Chapter
13

Teddy Bear Party (Ages 2-9)

Young children love the idea of bringing their teddy bears to a party, and once you have a room full of bears, your room has practically decorated itself!

Invitations

☆ Attach tiny teddy bears to teddy bear shaped invitations. Ask the children to bring their favorite teddy to the party. (If they don't have one, any stuffed animal will do.)

Attire

☆ The children will wear their teddy bear hats during the party (see Amusements).

Decorations

* Greet the children at the front door with a "stuffed bear" sitting in a lawn chair (made of a pair of overalls, shirt, tie, boots, all stuffed with wadded-up newspaper and the head of a real teddy bear sticking out from the shirt's collar).

* Round up all the teddy bears you can find, tie ribbons around their necks and helium balloons to their wrists. Set them around the room—sitting in a rocking chair, peeking out from behind a sofa, or clustered three together as a table centerpiece.

Amusements

* Teddy bear hats—Provide several colors of construction paper or light poster board, stickers, crayons, felt-tip markers, scissors, and glue. If the children are young, help them cut out crowns or hats, one for each child and one for the bear the child brought to the party.

* Pass the teddy—Divide the children into two teams. The first child in each line must put a teddy bear (the bigger the better) under his or her chin and pass it to the next child in line, who grabs it with his or her chin, and so forth, until it arrives at the end of the line. If the teddy is dropped, the team must start over. The first team to pass the teddy from the front to the back of the line without dropping it wins.

* Play Musical Teddies—This is traditional musical chairs (see Chapter 4), except that instead of the children sitting in the chairs, they place their teddies in the chairs instead.

Edibles

* Provide a picnic lunch in the backyard or serve barbecued hot dogs, chili and red gelatin salad.

* Make teddy bear shaped cookies from sugar cookie dough.

* Decorate the birthday cake with miniature teddy bears sitting with "gifts" in their laps (tiny boxes made by gift-wrapping sugar cubes).

Prizes and favors

* Tiny stuffed bears, teddy bear hats, *Goldilocks and the Three Bears* coloring books, story books, or puzzles.

Chapter

14

Circus Party (Ages 3-6)

A circus is an easy and affordable theme for a children's party.

Invitations

☆ Enclose invitations inside boxes of animal cookies, which can be hand-delivered or sent through the mail (ask the children to come dressed as clowns, tightrope walkers, or any circus performers).

☆ Make copies of a picture of a clown. Print the invitation on the back of the copies. Cut the pictures into jigsaw puzzles and mail. (Cut the pictures into a few pieces for small children and a dozen or more for older children.) The child will have the fun of assembling the puzzle in order to read the invitation.

Attire

★ Dress up as the ring master of the circus.

★ The children will be dressed as clowns or other circus performers.

Decorations

★ Set up a cardboard ticket booth at the front door.

★ A circus theme needs lots of color: balloons, crepe paper streamers, and stuffed animals—the bigger the better.

★ Create a circus tent indoors by attaching the center of a sheet to the center of the ceiling, suspending the corners of the sheet from the ceiling with fishing line. Add a cluster of balloons to each corner of the tent.

★ Create a circus tent outdoors by using a camping canopy decorated with crepe paper streamers and helium balloons.

★ Hang circus posters and banners.

★ Place the birthday cake in the center of the table, covered by a circus tent made from crepe paper streamers that hang down from a light fixture or the ceiling.

Amusements

★ Play circus calliope music during the party.

★ Hire a professional clown (be sure to ask for references). Note: if your guests are 3 years old or younger, it may be a good idea to have the clown put on his costume and makeup in front of the children, so they won't be frightened by the finished product.

★ Paint clown faces on the children, then take instant photos they can bring home with them as party favors.

★ Provide red clown noses for each guest to wear throughout the party. The noses may also be taken home as party favors.

☆ Borrow or buy exercise mats. Have the children perform circus acrobatics by tumbling, doing somersaults, cartwheels, etc.

☆ Have a circus parade around the house or yard.

☆ Near the end of the party, ask the guests to join you in playing a little joke on the birthday boy or girl. Come after the child with a bucket of water—tell him or her that it's water and you're going to dump it on his or her head. Then, of course, the water turns out to be confetti.

☆ Hire a balloon artist to make balloon animals for the children to take home as party favors.

Edibles

☆ Serve foods you would find at a circus—corn dogs, hot dogs, caramel corn, mini-donuts, peanuts, popcorn, and cotton candy (packaged cotton candy is available in the candy aisle in many grocery stores).

☆ Transform an ordinary round cake into a clown face. Draw a face using tubes of red, brown, and pink frosting. Squeeze on big, red, smiling lips, pink rouged cheeks, and brown bushy eyebrows. Crisscross small pieces of dark licorice over brown frosting eyes. Use a red strawberry, red ball, or a red clown's nose for the nose. Curl red crinkle ribbon for hair. Flatten a child's birthday hat for a hat. Make a collar from bright green, gathered tulle netting. Cut a bow tie out of a child's birthday hat.

☆ Serve clown cones (an upside-down ice cream cone served in a saucer with jelly bean eyes and black licorice lips and eyebrows).

Prizes and favors

☆ Clown makeup, balloon animals, clown noses, instant photos.

Chapter

15

Ballerina Party (Ages 3-6)

L ittle girls love to wear tutus and dance around the house like balle-
rinas, so why not fashion a party around this adorable theme?

Invitations

☆ Send ready-made invitations that are wearing tutus you
have made out of gathered tulle netting. Cut strips of pink
tulle measuring approximately 2 x 12 inches.
Gather them using a large needle and
pink carpet thread. Tie the tutus
around the invitations. Ask the
children to wear leotards or
swimsuits to the party.

Attire

* ☆ Greet the children at the door wearing a dance outfit, consisting of a leotard with a gathered tulle net tutu ruffle at the waist, colored leggings, ballet shoes and a tiara on your head.
* ☆ Make a pastel-colored tulle net tutu for each girl. Cut tulle into 12-by-36-inch pieces. Gather them at the waist using a large upholstery needle and colored string. Leave extra string at each end to tie around the girls' waists as they arrive.

Decorations

* ☆ Ballerina Cake centerpiece. (Use the Barbie Doll Cake recipe in Chapter 73 and add a pink ruffled tutu as the skirt.)
* ☆ Suspend pink crepe paper streamers from the ceiling over the table, attaching the streamers to the corners of the table.

Amusements

* ☆ Make up the girls' faces, pin their hair up, and add a tiara to each girl's head. (See U.S. Toy Company catalog in Resources.)
* ☆ Have a friend or dance professional give the girls a brief ballet lesson.
* ☆ Arrange the children in a circle and have them dance to the "Waltz of the Sugar Plum Fairies" from the *Nutcracker Suite.*
* ☆ Take the girls on a ballerina parade around the block (they'll enjoy showing off their costumes).
* ☆ Videotape the festivities and show the tape near the end of the party.

Edibles

* ☆ Serve Tutu Balls (see Snowball Ice Cream recipe in Chapter 73 made with tinted pink coconut) with the Ballerina Cake.

Prizes and favors

* ☆ Ballerina dolls, tutus, makeup kits, tiaras, ballerina coloring books.

Chapter

16

Fireman Party (Ages 3-6)

Many young children dream of growing up to become firemen. This party will help them fulfill their dreams.

Invitations

☆ Attach miniature fire trucks to ready-made invitations. Hand deliver them or enclose in small boxes and send through the mail. Ask the children to wear their rain boots and slickers to the party.

Attire

☆ Greet the children at the door wearing a fireman's outfit, consisting of black pants and boots, red suspenders, a rain slicker, and a bright red fire hat.

59

☆   Purchase red fire hats at your 98-cent store or party supply store. As the children arrive, place the fire hats on their heads.

Decorations

☆   Fireman Cake centerpiece (see Edibles setion).

☆   Suspend red crepe paper streamers from the ceiling to look like flames.

☆   Decorate the room with stuffed Dalmatians, toy fire truck, fire hats, and red fire hydrants.

Amusements

☆   Visit your local firehouse in advance and ask if they could send one of their fire trucks to the party to give rides to the children. Usually, they are glad to help out, unless they are on a call. Otherwise, ask if you can bring the children to the station during the party for a mini field trip so they can sit in the fire truck and get a tour of the firehouse. Often, the children will be given fire safety coloring books as mementos of their visit.

☆   If the party takes place in the summer, ask the children to bring their swimsuits so they can play in the fire hydrant sprinkler. These sprinklers are available at many toy stores.

☆   Play Fireman Says (a version of Simon Says).

☆   Play Stomp Out the Fire—Inflate balloons and write each guest's name on three balloons. Place the inflated balloons under a king-sized sheet or plastic tarp that has been masking-taped to the floor. Explain to the children that the balloons are a fire that must be stomped out. They are to break every balloon but one. The guest whose name is on the last balloon is declared the winner and is given a prize.

☆   Videotape all the activities and show the tape near the end of the party.

Edibles

☆   Serve Fireman Hero Sandwiches (see Chapter 72) and potato chips.

☆   To make a Fireman Cake, decorate a birthday cake with a miniature fire truck, a fire hydrant, and a tiny Dalmatian dog. Serve with rocky road ice cream.

Prizes and favors

☆   Toy fire trucks, fireman hats, plastic or stuffed Dalmatian dogs, fireman coloring books.

Wild Animal Party (Ages 3-10)

 Wild Animal Party can be held inside your house, in a backyard, at a park, or at the zoo (where it actually becomes a destination party).

Invitations

☆ Attach the invitations to the wrists or necks of small stuffed animals, such as tiny brown bears. Ask each child to bring his or her favorite stuffed animal to the party.

☆ Send each child a mask that you have cut out of colored cardboard or paper plates. Print the invitation on the back of the mask. Ask the children to decorate their masks to look like wild animals and wear them to the party.

61

Attire

* Dress in bush gear: khaki shorts and shirts, hiking boots with thick socks, and pith helmets.

Decorations

* Cut out large brown felt animal footprints, and have them walking into the house from the front walkway. (Use two-sided tape to secure them.)
* Cover the front door with animal cage bars (hang strips of floor-length black crepe paper).
* Drape nets from the ceiling.
* Hang posters of Africa and wild animals.
* Decorate the serving table and the room with stuffed animals—the bigger and wilder, the better.
* Place large stuffed animals inside two or three large cages made from cardboard appliances boxes. (Cut out bars on one side or make a square opening in the front of box and string black crepe paper strips to form the bars.)
* Drape snakes over furniture, up and around artificial plants or trees. (Stuff the legs of old panty hose with rags or crushed paper. Sew the open ends closed. Glue on red jelly bean eyes and a red felt tongue.)
* Set clusters of helium-filled animal balloons around the room or yard.

Amusements

* Peanut Zoo—The children can create their own Peanut Zoos by converting ordinary in-shell peanuts into animals. Provide each child with a sack of peanuts and 20 to 30 colored pipe cleaners. They can twist the pipe cleaners around the peanuts to make legs, horns, and tails. The faces of the animals can be created with felt-tip markers or poster paint. This project can get a little messy, so seat the children at a table covered with a plastic disposable tablecloth.
* Wild Animal Obstacle Challenge—Create an obstacle course for your wild animals (the children) to traverse. Each child needs to decide which wild animal he or she wants to be—a lion, elephant, tiger, etc. Then he or she is off to conquer the course. Send only one child through at a time so the others can enjoy watching. The course can begin in the house and extend onto the patio or into the yard. For obstacles, suspend wooden

boards over make-believe dangerous rivers and around bushes and trees where dangerous animals (large stuffed animals) are lurking. Connect cardboard boxes for the children to jump over or into.

✯ Animal Charades—This game is played like regular charades except that the children must imitate an animal. Folded animal pictures are drawn from a basket. The first child who guesses which animal is being depicted gets to be the next contestant. The game goes on until every child has had a turn.

✯ Blind Man's Animal Art—This is similar to animal charades except that the animals are drawn instead of acted out. You will need a blindfold, an easel, a large pad of drawing paper, and a felt-tip pen. Divide the group into two teams. Blindfold a member from one team at a time and have him or her try to draw a certain animal for his team members to identify within three minutes. The teams alternate back and forth until each child has had a turn.

✯ Decorate Animal Masks—If you didn't send cardboard masks as invitations, as described above, let the children make their own animal masks during the party. Provide colored cardboard or paper plates, yarn, wallpaper and fabric scraps, glue, and scissors.

Edibles

✯ Serve Make-Your-Own Monkey Fruit Kabobs (thread banana and other fruit chunks onto wooden skewers), Animal Sandwiches (cut sandwiches into animal shapes using cookie cutters), and Dirt Pie (see Chapter 73).

✯ Animal crackers are a must, of course. Place one box at each place setting.

✯ Wild Animal Birthday Cake—arrange a group of plastic animals on top of the cake.

Prizes and favors

✯ Tiny stuffed animals, plastic zoo or farm animals, animal puzzles, posters, masks, or puppets.

Make Believe Party (Ages 3-11)

Kids love to play dress-up, so a Make Believe Party is a winning theme from the start. They like to pretend they are grown-ups, of course, but they also like to dress up as cowboys, Indians, astronauts, hula dancers, karate masters, or movie or video game heros.

Invitations

☆ Purchase a book of paper dolls, punch out the clothes, and print the invitation on the back of each outfit.

Attire

☆ As hostess, you should wear a humorous outfit in the spirit of make-believe. For example, you can don an evening gown, embellished with costume jewelry and a sparkly crown.

Decorations

☆ Decorate with clothes racks full of dress-up clothes and costumes, plus baskets filled with hats, shoes, canes, umbrellas, shawls, scarves, feather boas, top hats, wigs, long or bow ties, helmets, swords, a bride's veil, capes, purses, and so on. Raid your local Goodwill or thrift store, or ask the children's parents to contribute to the cause. Be sure clothes and accessories from parents are identified with tags or markings so they can be returned after the party.

☆ Decorate the serving table with dolls that are all dressed up. Add a few extras, such as strings of sequins for Barbie and a black top hat for Ken.

☆ Provide one or two full-length mirrors, decorated with balloons and streamers.

Amusements

☆ Provide stations manned by four of your friends who have agreed to serve as makeup artist, manicurist, hair stylist, and jewelry coordinator. Round up plenty of costume jewelry, makeup, nail polish and fake nails, plus hot rollers and hair spray for exotic makeovers. The children will line up at each station, anxious to receive their mustaches, beards, long, decorated fingernails, glittery up-dos, glamorous jewelry, and so on.

☆ Spray the girls with perfume or cologne and splash a little after-shave cologne on the boys.

☆ Make a runway for the guests to model their attire once they are all dressed up.

☆ Video tape the guests as they go up and down the runway. Take plenty of instant photos as well. The video can be shown near the end of the party and the photos can be taken home as party favors.

Edibles

✮ Serve "grown-up" party foods on "grown-up" serving platters, such as finger sandwiches, cocktail weiners, fancy hors d'oeuvres, and canapes. Serve ginger ale in long-stemmed, plastic champagne glasses.

✮ Decorate the birthday cake with paper dolls and their clothes.

Prizes and favors

✮ Cologne, child's necklace or bracelet, gold or silver crowns, instant photos.

Tea Party (Ages 4-7)

This is an elegant dress-up party for little girls.

Invitations

☆ Write the invitation on the center of an 8" white doily and mail in square envelopes.

Decorations

☆ Set up a child's table and chair set with a child's tea set and teddy bear or doll

67

guests. Spread the table with a lace or embroidered linen cloth and a fresh flower centerpiece arranged in a tea pot. Tie lace ribbons at the bears' necks or dress up the dolls in their finest attire.

☆ Add displays of fancy gloves, hats, hand mirrors, old-fashioned fans, pocketbooks, and jewelry.

☆ Set the guests' table with a lace tablecloth, napkins, china tea sets, and your finest silver tableware. Arrange a fresh flower centerpiece for this table as well.

☆ Place elegant, white, satin-finish place cards at each place setting (use black ink and a calligraphy pen to write the girls' names).

☆ Pin a mini-corsage on the birthday girl (thread the stems of three small flowers through the center of a white paper doily, wrap the stems with a second doily, and tie with a narrow satin acetate ribbon).

Amusements

☆ The tea party itself will be the primary activity. Make it last as long as you can by presenting the various delicacies one at a time.

☆ After the tea party, have a makeover artist (one of your friends, perhaps) make up the girls with makeup, new up-do hairstyles and fancy jewelry. Purchase inexpensive makeup for each girl and let the girls take their makeup home as party favors.

☆ Take instant photos of each girl after her makeover (standing beside the birthday girl) and send the photos home as remembrances of the party.

☆ You can also include a few civilized and proper tea party games, such as Telephone or the Spoon Race (see Chapter 4).

☆ After the games, the birthday girl may open her gifts and award door prizes (the girls who have stickers under their chairs are the winners).

☆ Videotape the party and show the tape near the end of the party.

Edibles

☆ Serve a proper tea with a selection of these delicacies:

- Scones (use scone mix, available at your supermarket).

- Cream puffs, tarts, and hot-cross buns.

- Spiced pears.

- Cold cheeses.

- Chocolate-dipped fresh strawberries.
- Chocolate truffles.
- Decaffeinated tea (or apple juice) poured from an elegant tea pot.

★ Or, try making these tea sandwiches:

1. Spread softened butter over pieces of thinly sliced bread.
2. Add sandwich fillings:
   - *Ham and Swiss cheese* (thinly sliced and garnished with Dijon mustard).
   - *Walnuts and cream cheese* (whip one package softened cream cheese together with 1/4 cup cream until smooth. Add 1/2 cup finely diced celery and 1/2 cup chopped walnuts).
   - *Pineapple and cream cheese* (whip together one package cream cheese with 1/2 cup cream. Add one cup well-drained crushed pineapple).
3. Wrap and refrigerate the sandwiches.
4. Shortly before serving, remove from the refrigerator, trim off the crusts and cut into circles, hearts, and other fancy shapes that can be made with cookie cutters.

★ Serve an elegant round birthday cake, topped with fresh flowers, lace, and narrow ribbons (dangling over the edge of the cake onto the table).

Prizes and favors

★ Child's jewelry, plastic tea sets, makeup kits, nail polish, nail glitter, instant photos.

Tip

★ Remember, these little girls have been serving tea to their dolls for years, so they'll enjoy the real thing. You'll need to play the roll to the hilt—dress up for the occasion and serve with great ceremony. This will make the girls feel like elegant little ladies!

Chapter

20

Indy 500 Party (Ages 4-7)
===

ere's a chance for the kids to build their own race cars and drive them in the big race. You'll need to round up one good-sized cardboard box per child, but it will be worth it when you see how easily your guests are entertained during the party.

Invitations

☆ Attach miniature race cars to ready-made invitations. Hand deliver them or enclose in small boxes and send through the mail. Ask the children to wear their bicycle or skateboarding helmets and safety or ski goggles to the party.

Attire

☆ The children will wear their "racing helmets" and "racing goggles" when they drive their cars in the race.

70

Decorations

 ✸   Decorate a rectangular cake with an oval racetrack and miniature race
      cars. Add crossed black and white checkered flags on the front of the
      cake. (Use black felt-tipped marker to draw squares on white paper flags.)
 ✸   Suspend black and white crepe paper streamers from the ceiling, attach-
      ing the ends to the corners of the serving table.
 ✸   Decorate the walls with racing posters or large black and white check-
      ered flags.

Amusements

 ✸   Give each child one appliance-sized cardboard box, such as a dishwasher,
      TV, or microwave box. Also provide stickers, broad markers, large cray-
      ons, and such accessories as tires and steering wheels (colored plastic
      plates), headlights (small aluminum pie plates), and windshield wipers
      (wooden chopsticks). This can be a messy project, so you might want to
      take it outside or to the garage. The children decorate their cars with
      racing stripes (brightly colored plastic tape), numbers, their names and
      sponsor's logos, such as a cat's face for Wild Cat Motor Oil, and so forth.
      Once the cars are decorated, they can be accessorized by stapling or
      taping on the tires, steering wheels, lights and windshield wipers.
 ✸   When the children have finished building their cars, they don their helmets
      and goggles, climb in (stand inside their boxes, holding onto the sides), and
      race around the block. Use checkered flags to declare the winner(s) and hand
      out prizes to all the children, whether they won or not.
 ✸   Videotape all the activities and show the tape as the children enjoy the
      cake and ice cream.

Edibles

 ✸   Serve the decorated cake, described above,
      along with rocky road ice cream.

Prizes and favors

 ✸   The cardboard race cars they make dur-
      ing the party, racing post-
      ers, small plastic or metal
      race cars, instant photos.

Chapter

21

Dinosaur Party (Ages 4-8)

K ids are just crazy about dinosaurs. Here's a party dedicated to all things prehistoric.

Invitations

☆ Attach the invitations to small toy dinosaurs or "dinosaur bones" (dried beef bones).

Attire

☆ Dress in caveman costumes, complete with clubs.

Decorations

✯ Cut large brown felt dinosaur footprints and have them leading into the house from the front walkway. (Use two-sided tape to secure them.)

✯ Create a dinosaur centerpiece for your table by forming defrosted bread dough into the shape of a dinosaur (use kitchen scissors to form a jagged spine.) Set plastic toy dinosaurs beside the centerpiece, standing amidst large rocks you've hauled in from your yard, plus old steak bones and a few dinosaur footprints cut from dark brown felt.

✯ Place stuffed toy dinosaurs around the room, peering out from behind a plant or piece of furniture. Set the largest one at the front door to welcome the guests.

Amusements

✯ Dinosaur Play Dough Contest—Provide store-bought or homemade play dough (see recipe in Chapter 5) for the children to use to create their own take-home dinosaurs. Be sure to have several plastic or rubber dinosaurs available for them to use as models.

✯ Dinosaur Race—See wheelbarrow race in Chapter 3.

✯ Dinosaur Coloring Contest—Purchase dinosaur coloring books. Let each child select one page to color. Give prizes.

✯ Dinosaur Egg Hunt—Similar to an Easter egg hunt, except that you hide dinosaur eggs (plastic Easter eggs filled with dinosaur Gummi candies). Variation: hide the eggs or small plastic dinosaurs in the sand box.

✯ Dinosaur Mural—Use masking tape to attach a long roll of brown wrapping paper to a wall. Give the children crayons and let them draw dinosaurs and cavemen. Or, they can sit at the table and use felt-tip markers to draw on a plastic tablecloth.

✯ Make a caveman piñata by stuffing a brown grocery sack with crushed paper and candies. Suspend the piñata from a tree branch and let the children swing away. Tip: Have an extra supply of candy on hand for anyone who wasn't quick on the pick-up.

☆ If you need a rainy day activity, let the kids build a dinosaur cave by draping sheets, blankets and quilts over the furniture. Let the children eat Dinosaur Sandwiches and Dinosaur Teeth (see Edibles section) inside their cave.

☆ Videotape or photograph the children in their costumes.

☆ Show a rented Flintstones movie.

Edibles

☆ Caveman Finger Foods—barbecued dinosaur legs (chicken or turkey drumsticks), and barbecued dinosaur ribs (baked beef ribs).

☆ Dinosaur Sandwiches—peanut butter and jelly on white bread, cut into dinosaur shapes with a dinosaur cookie cutter.

☆ Decorate the birthday cake with small plastic toy dinosaurs. Stick their legs down into the cake.

☆ Prehistoric Volcano Punch—fruit punch with scoops of raspberry sherbet, topped with cold raspberry soda pop, which will make the sherbet fizz, creating a volcano effect.

☆ Dinosaur Teeth—candy corn.

Prizes and favors

☆ Toy dinosaurs, dinosaur stickers, and coloring books.

King/Queen for a Day (Ages 4-8)

child absolutely loves the idea of being king or queen for a day. Go all out and take advantage of the theme to praise your child and build his or her self-esteem.

Invitations

☆ Cut crowns large enough to fit around a child's head from yellow poster board. Glue ends together. Cover with spray glue and sprinkle with silver glitter. Handprint the invitation on the back of the crown and mail in a padded envelope. Ask the children to wear their crowns to the party.

Attire

☆ Go to your fabric store and purchase a couple of yards of gold metallic fabric, which can be fashioned into a regal cape for your child to wear throughout the party, along with a glittery crown and scepter.

Decorations

☆ Create more sparkly yellow poster board crowns, and place them on dolls and stuffed animals. Arrange the dolls and stuffed animals into a royal court circle on a table.

☆ The children will wear their sparkly crowns (the party invitations), which will add even more glitter to the party. Have several extra crowns on hand for those children who forgot to bring their crowns to the party.

Amusements

☆ Play The Queen Says or The King Says, a variation of Simon Says. The birthday boy or girl reigns over this game, of course.

☆ Play Musical Royal Scepter, which is the same game as Musical Chairs (see Chapter 4), except that the children remain seated and pass around a scepter. When the music stops, the child holding the scepter is out of the game. Make the scepter by attaching a large star to the end of a 12" dowel, covering it with spray glue, and sprinkling it with silver glitter.

Edibles

☆ Serve a birthday cake decorated with a scepter made of icing and the words Happy Birthday, [child's name]—King [or Queen] for a Day.

☆ Serve Royal Jewel Treats—plastic cups of red gelatin topped with red and gold jelly beans (jewels).

☆ Make Royal Punch—red fruit punch with raspberry sherbet, topped with cold lemon-lime soda.

Prizes and favors

☆ Costume jewelry, gold or silver crowns, home-made scepters, instant photos.

Chapter
23

Cowboy or Cowgirl BBQ (Ages 4-8)

*T*his is an easy party to plan—all you need is to add a few Wild West decorations to an ordinary barbecue lunch or dinner, and you'll have a winner!

Invitations

☆ Cut out invitations in the shape of cowboy hats and hand-print the party information on the back of the hats. You can also use a computer graphics program to create a customized invitation that includes clip art, such as cowboy hats, cowboy boots, a cactus, a saddle, or any other appropriate symbol.

Attire

★ Dress in full Western style—jeans, boots, cowboy hats, red bandanas, even fake spurs, which you can find at a costume or novelty shop.

Decorations

★ Decorate your home, yard, or patio with bales of hay, saddles, branding irons, and potted cactus plants.

★ Cover your serving table with a red checkered tablecloth. Your centerpiece can be a hay-filled cowboy hat with a little cowboy or cowgirl peeking out (a doll wearing a cowboy hat and a red bandana).

Amusements

★ Play Pin the Tail on the Donkey.

★ Have a Roping Contest. Make a lasso by tying a slipknot in a piece of rope. Have the children take turns trying to lasso the horns of a bull—that is, the handlebars of a bicycle. (Cover the bicycle with a blanket, leaving only the handlebars showing.)

★ Play Horseshoes in the backyard (lightweight plastic horseshoe games are available at toy stores).

★ Have a hayride for the children (hire a horse and wagon), or borrow a pick-up truck and fill the back with bales of hay.

Edibles

★ Serve barbecued hamburgers and hot dogs, chili, corn on the cob, baked beans with brown sugar, potato chips, and cowboy or cowgirl hot chocolate—hot chocolate served in a mug with a red bandana tied around the handle. The children may keep these bandanas as party favors.

★ Decorate the birthday cake with toy horses, fencing, and miniature bales of hay.

Prizes and favors

★ Bandanas, cowboy hats, toy spurs, or favors made by filling miniature cowboy hats with trail mix made from M&M's, peanuts, and raisins. Wrap in cellophane and tie with a ribbon.

Chapter

24

October Pumpkin Party (Ages 4-10)

This is an easy and practical party to plan for a birthday that falls during the month of October.

Invitations

☆ Handprint the invitations on orange construction paper using black felt-tip markers. Roll them into scrolls, tie with black ribbons, and insert inside small plastic pumpkins (or attach to fresh pumpkins with a push pin). Hand-deliver, or carefully pack and mail.

Attire

☆ Ask the children to come dressed as pumpkins—wearing orange clothing, green hats, and jack-o'-lantern faces painted on with black eyebrow pencil or face paint. Encourage their parents to use their imaginations when helping the children get into costume.

Decorations

☆ Decorate the room with orange balloons (with jack-o'-lantern faces drawn with black marker), plus orange and black crepe paper streamers.

☆ Place jack-o'-lanterns around the room.

Amusements

☆ Hold a pumpkin decorating contest. Provide one small pumpkin per child, along with felt, fabric scraps, markers, construction paper, carrots, dried fruits, jelly beans, and plastic toothpicks. Give the children plenty of time to decorate their pumpkins. Give prizes for the scariest, silliest, cutest, etc. Of course, the children may take their pumpkins home as party favors.

☆ Mr. Pumpkin Musical Chairs—This is played the same way as the regular game (see Chapter 4), except that the children stay seated and pass a small decorated pumpkin around the circle as the music plays. The child who is caught holding the pumpkin when the music stops is out of the game. The last child left is declared the winner.

Edibles

☆ Make Pumpkin Sugar Cookies by decorating round sugar cookies with orange frosting and using black licorice to make eyes, nose, and mouth.

☆ Serve Pumpkin Punch—Fill a large, hollowed-out pumpkin with any orange juice drink and scoops of orange sherbet. Pour cold orange soda over the mixture, causing a spooky foaming effect.

☆ Have a birthday cake decorated with a picture of a jack-o'-lantern whose teeth form letters spelling out Happy Birthday.

Prizes and favors

☆ Small plastic pumpkins filled with candy corn, pumpkin face lollipops, Halloween sticker books or coloring books.

Somewhere Over the Rainbow Party (Ages 4-11)

This theme is based on the movie *The Wizard of Oz*, which opens up a world of possibilities when it comes to decorating, food, games, and activities.

Invitations

☆ Send invitations attached to small net bags filled with gold coin candies, or create your own invitations by drawing rainbows on the front of each, using colored crayons. (The colors of the rainbow are red, orange, yellow, green, blue, indigo, and violet.)

Decorations

☆ Use butcher paper and tempera paint to create a giant rainbow, and hang it over the entryway door as the guests arrive.

☆ Create a rainbow and pot of gold as a table centerpiece. Run strips of colored crepe-paper along the center of the table and into a small terra cotta flowerpot sprayed with gold paint and filled to overflowing with gold coin candies.

☆ Hang balloons and crepe-paper streamers in rainbow colors, or draw rainbows on plain white balloons, using wide markers.

☆ Place a package of rainbow stickers at each place setting as party favors.

Amusements

☆ Pot of Gold Treasure Hunt—Create a treasure map that leads the children from one clue to another throughout the yard, until they finally come to the pot of gold, a small, gold-sprayed coffee can filled with gold coin candies, or actual pennies, nickels, or quarters. When the children find the treasure, divide the coins up equally. (Count the coins ahead of time so everyone will get an even share.)

☆ Play Pin the Pot of Gold on the Rainbow, which is played the same way as Pin the Tail on the Donkey.

Edibles

☆ Serve Rainbow Sandwiches—triple-deckers, made by alternating white and pumpernickel bread with raspberry jelly and layers of whipped cream cheese (colored with blue food coloring.) Slice each sandwich into four horizontal strips, held together with fancy food picks that have colored cellophane ruffles at the ends. Serve with potato chips.

☆ Rainbow Surprise—A mug filled with a single scoop of raspberry sherbet with cold lemon-lime soda poured over the top. (The surprise is that the drink will foam.)

☆ "Rainbow Cake" – Bake a three-layer cake whose layers are each a different color (use food coloring). Using squeeze-tube frosting, create a rainbow on the cake that ends at a gold-sprayed small can filled to overflowing with gold coin candies. (Let the candies spill over onto the cake.)

Prizes and favors

☆ Rainbow crayons, rainbow stickers, gold coin candies.

Wet 'n Wild Water Party (Ages 4-12)

This is a great party theme for a hot summer's day. If you don't have a swimming pool, you can still provide lots of splash by using the ideas in this chapter.

Invitations

☆ Write the invitations on inexpensive deflated beach balls. Inflate and deliver, or mail deflated in padded envelopes. Ask the children to wear their swimsuits to the party and bring towels and changes of clothes for later.

Attire

★ Swimsuits.

Decorations

★ Dress the largest stuffed animals you can find in swim wear, with swim goggles, visors, and thongs. Set them on lawn chairs covered with beach towels.

Amusements

★ Swimming—If you have a pool, the main activity will be swimming, of course. Kids will make their own fun—just provide plastic balls, Noodles (long foam tubes that can be bent into different shapes), a net for water volleyball, rafts, and rings.

★ Water Slide—If you don't have a pool, an alternate activity is splashing and sliding down a long, wet, slippery plastic slide on the ground. You can buy one of these slides for about $20. You keep it wet and slippery by either attaching it to your garden hose or running the sprinkler over it.

★ Water Balloon Contest—Draw a bull's-eye on your back fence and let the children throw water balloons at it. Each child has three tries. A prize goes to the child with the most bull's-eyes.

★ Water Balloon Volleyball—Play volleyball using a water balloon instead of a standard volleyball. Of course, you'll need to have a supply of water balloons ready as they break throughout the game.

★ Squirt Gun Balloon Race—Provide each child with a squirt gun and an air-filled balloon. If you have a swimming pool, line the children up on one side of the pool and have them squirt their balloons to the other side. The first child whose balloon reaches the other side wins. If you don't have a swimming pool, you may use a wading pool, with the children competing one at a time, squirting the balloon across the wading pool to a mark on the opposite side. Use a stop watch to determine which child's balloon reaches the designated mark in the least amount of time.

✸ Wet Marble Contest—Place 15 or 20 marbles in the bottom of a bucket or tub of water. Set your timer. Each child gets one minute to pick up as many marbles as possible with his or her toes and place them on the ground. The child who manages to pick up the most marbles gets to keep all the marbles as a prize.

✸ Sea Shell Hunt—Hide sea shells in the sand box ahead of time. At a signal, see which child can find the most shells in a certain length of time.

✸ Put Out the Fire—Divide the group into two teams, and designate a team leader for each one. Each team should line up single-file. Place a bucket of water in front of each team. Give each leader a metal cup that he or she must fill with water from the bucket and pass down the line to the last team member, who empties whatever water is left into a two-quart plastic bowl. Then the cup is sent back to the front of the line to be filled again. The process continues until one team's bowl is full; that team wins the game.

✸ Water War—Convert empty plastic soda bottles into water guns by making holes in the plastic caps and filling the bottles with water. Provide each child with his own water gun, and the children will be ready to squirt each other in a water war.

Edibles

✸ Serve birthday cake, along with Jell-O Jigglers, Peanut Butter Banana Dogs, and s'mores (see Chapters 72 and 73).

Prizes and favors

✸ Soda bottle water guns, Noodles, sea shells, water toys.

Chapter

27

Petting Zoo Party (Ages 4-12)

This party requires live animals, so you'll need to borrow them, rent them, or have the guests bring their own. The pets can be anything from gold fish to turtles to horses—the more, the better!

Invitations

☆ Attach tiny stuffed animals to the invitations, such as dogs, cats, horses, rabbits, and so forth. Hand deliver or mail in small boxes. Ask the guests to dress casually and to bring their pets to the party. (Be sure to have them bring their own leashes, cages, water bowls, and food, if necessary.)

☆ Attach the invitations to real dog biscuits.

Attire

☆ Casual dress.

Decorations

✯ Decorate with posters of animals, a decorated dog house, sacks of animal food, and oversized baby bottles (can be purchased from a vet supply store).

✯ The animals themselves will decorate the rest of the party site!

Amusements

✯ Most of the time is spent petting the animals, riding the animals, if appropriate, and having Polaroid photos taken beside the animals (the photos are sent home with the guests as party favors).

✯ In many areas of the country you can rent petting zoos for the afternoon. They will bring their animals to your party, including ponies for pony rides.

✯ Ask your local pet store owner to provide a variety of pets for the party, such as puppies, kittens, or talking parrots.

✯ If appropriate, have a fetching contest or Frisbee toss for the dogs attending the party. Award prizes to the dogs' owners.

✯ Have the children dress up their pets for the party. Provide a supply of tulle netting (for tutus), ribbons, birthday hats, sun glasses, glittery crowns, and colorful fabrics (to make shirts, skirts, shorts, etc.) Award prizes for the funniest, most creative, silliest, etc.

✯ Videotape the party, from beginning to end. Show the tape near the end of the party while the kids are eating their cake and ice cream and the birthday child is opening gifts.

Edibles

✯ Decorate the birthday cake with tiny stuffed animals on leashes. Serve with ice cream and serve in dog dishes.

Prizes and favors

✯ Animal treats, cat or dog collars, animal coloring books, small plastic animals.

Chapter

28

Out-of-This-World Party (Ages 5-9)

This may also be called a Space Age Party, Astronaut Party, *Star Wars* Party, or *Star Trek* Party—whichever is most appropriate for the age group.

Invitations

☆ Spray-paint fist-sized rocks with silver paint. Write the words "official moon rock" on each rock with black permanent marker. Wrap each rock in silver tissue paper and mail it in a small square box with a party invitation.

Attire

☆ Ask the guests to come dressed as their favorite characters, depending on the party's theme. For example, if it's a *Star Wars*

Party, they can come dressed as Ewoks, Darth Vader, Storm Troopers, or Princess Leah. If it's a *Star Trek* party, they can dress as characters from the TV show, such as Spock, Captain Kirk, Scottie, or Mr. Sulu.

☆ Greet the children at the door dressed as your favorite character.

Decorations

☆ Display a "moon rock"— any large, impressive rock painted silver.

☆ Create the illusion of a night sky filled with stars and planets. Keep the lights low in your main party room, and illuminate the ceiling with a dozen or more strands of tiny white lights. To create planets, suspend various sizes of Styrofoam balls, sprayed with liquid glue and sprinkled with silver glitter.

☆ Use sheets of heavy duty aluminum foil to cover the serving table and furniture in the room.

☆ Make spaceships by spraying toilet paper tubes with silver paint and adding white cone-shaped coffee filters as noses, facing skyward. Set the space ships amidst the aluminum foil.

☆ Greet your guests at the door with a life-size Darth Vader, Yoda, or R2-D2, available through Advanced Graphics (see Resources.)

Amusements

☆ Show a *Star Wars* movie or a taped *Star Trek* episode.

☆ Play the Flying Saucer Game: Place an upside-down Frisbee on the floor. Let the children take turns tossing six asteroids (small bean bags) into the flying saucer from 10 feet away. The contestant who lands the most asteroids inside the saucer is the winner. (Have a playoff in case of a tie.)

☆ If the party takes place after dark, borrow a good-quality telescope. Have the children take turns viewing planets, including the planet's moons or rings.

☆ If fireworks are allowed in your city, purchase a supply of sparklers ahead of time. Light one sparkler for each child to twirl in the sky.

☆ Play background music from *Star Wars* or *Star Trek* during the party.

☆ Play the I'm Going to Mars game if the children are 8 or 9 years old. The children sit in a circle, and one says, "I'm going to Mars and I'm going to take a [any item of the child's choice] with me." The next child repeats what the first child said, adding another item. This continues around the circle, resulting in giggles as each child tries to remember all the items the other children said.

☆ Make up a large batch of play dough (see Chapter 5) for the children to use to create a creature from outer space. Furnish a supply of odd buttons, pipe cleaners, wire, foil, bolts, washers, etc. for them to add to their creations. This will keep them occupied for about 20 minutes. You can give prizes if you like.

☆ A month or so before the party, save everything you can find that can be used for building spaceships: foil, frozen orange juice containers, paper towel and toilet paper tubes, small cereal boxes, and so on. Divide the materials you've collected into three or four piles, along with tape, a stapler, scissors, paper clips, and felt-tip markers. Assign a group of children to each pile, and see which one can build the best spaceship.

Edibles

☆ Pass out Milky Way candy bars for the children to eat while watching the video.

☆ Serve "space food," such as powdered orange drink, dried fruits, beef jerky, or actual freeze-dried foods purchased from an outdoor recreation supply store.

☆ Decorate a cake to resemble the moon by spreading the frosting in a lumpy, wavy pattern. Set a plastic astronaut figurine on top of the cake, beside a small American flag. If you have a spaceship to place next to the cake, all the better. Add small spray-painted silver rocks to the cake display. Darken the room and use lighted sparklers instead of candles.

   Variation: Top your "moon" with moon people (large green gumdrops with red toothpick arms and legs and three eyes made by pressing red hot candies across their foreheads).

Prizes and favors

☆ Plastic aliens or astronauts, stick-on glow-in-the-dark stars, toy telescopes, and star and space stickers.

Frosty the Snowman Party (Ages 5-9)

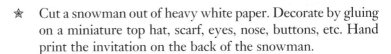

T his is a popular party theme.

Invitations

   ✫   Cut a snowman out of heavy white paper. Decorate by gluing on a miniature top hat, scarf, eyes, nose, buttons, etc. Hand print the invitation on the back of the snowman.

Attire

   ✫   If the children will be out in the snow, ask the parents to send along their warm snowsuits, hats, scarves, mittens, and waterproof snow boots.

Decorations

☆ Build a real snowman in the front yard, ready to greet the guests as they arrive. If you don't live in snow country, or if the party is during warm weather, place a store-bought snowman lawn ornament out in the yard.

☆ Sprinkle fake snow or place a roll of cotton along the center of the serving table as a base for tiny snowmen that can be made by gluing three small Styrofoam balls together and decorating in the traditional way.

☆ Place clusters of white helium balloons around the room.

Amusements

☆ Snowman Contest—Divide the children into groups of three or four each and let them build small snowmen out of the snow in your yard (if there is any). Let the children color their snowmen using spray bottles filled with colored water (plain water with food coloring added.) Provide them with scarves, raisins, carrots, pieces of charcoal, large buttons, and so forth. Take instant photos of each guest standing next to his decorated snowman and send the photos home as party favors. Give prizes to the team who made and decorated the funniest, most creative or meanest snowman.

☆ Snowball Hunt—Hide snowballs (popcorn balls wrapped in cellophane) around the yard. Provide each child with a white decorated lunch bag for the hunt.

Edibles

☆ Provide a winter weather menu—serve Frosty the Snowman Chili or Frosty the Snowman Stew (chili or stew straight out of the can), hot dogs, chips and hot chocolate, served with plenty of miniature "snowballs" (mini-marshmallows) and "snow" (whipped cream).

☆ Decorate the birthday cake with a miniature Frosty the Snowman (made with giant marshmallows held together with a long cocktail or bamboo skewer).

Prizes and favors

☆ The snowballs (popcorn balls) they found during the snowball hunt, scarves, mittens, Frosty the Snowman coloring or story books, instant photos.

Baby Doll Shower (Ages 5-10)

T his is a pretend baby shower where the children bring their baby dolls to a shower.

Invitations

☆ Attach baby rattles to the birthday invitations and mail in padded envelopes. Ask each girl to bring a baby doll and a doll-size or regular high chair, crib, rocking chair, playpen, stroller, swing, or car seat.

Attire

☆ Pin a corsage on each girl as she arrives for the party. Make each corsage out of one silk flower, one baby pacifier, and ribbon.

Decorations

☆ Ba-ba Bundt Cake centerpiece (see Edibles section).

☆ Suspend a decorated pastel-colored umbrella over the table, with pink streamers hanging down. Decorate the umbrella with ruffled crepe paper, tulle netting, ribbons, and silk flowers.

☆ Set the table with baby shower paper goods: a pink and blue tablecloth, napkins, plates, and cups.

☆ Ask the girls to set their babies up in the high chairs, cribs, and so forth that they brought with them to the party. Attach pink and blue helium balloons to the backs of the high chairs and the backs of the guests' chairs at the tables.

Amusements

☆ Insert small numbered pieces of paper inside the helium balloons tied to the backs of the guests' chairs. One at a time, have the girls burst their balloons (by sitting on them), then match their numbers with those attached to the baby shower gifts displayed under a decorated golf umbrella sitting on the floor. The gifts can be doll clothes, blankets, diapers, and so forth, that the girls may take home as party favors.

☆ Spoon race, using cotton balls (see Chapter 4).

☆ Musical Baby Dolls—This is traditional musical chairs (see Chapter 4) except that instead of the children sitting in the chairs, they place their dolls in the chairs.

☆ Potty Toss—Place a child's potty about 10 feet away from the contestant, who is given 10 diaper pins to toss into the potty, one at a time. The girl who tosses the most diaper pins into the potty wins.

☆ Baby Bottle Race—Furnish each girl with a small baby bottle (with nipple) filled with juice or water. When you say, "Go," the girls start sucking their bottles. The first one to empty her bottle wins.

★ Video tape the festivities and show the tape near the end of the party (they'll like the baby bottle race best).

Edibles

★ Serve Ba-ba Bundt Cake and ice cream. Frost a supermarket bundt cake. Fill a baby bottle with jelly beans and tie the neck of the bottle with a pink ribbon. Insert the bottle in the center hole of the bundt cake. Place birthday candles around the edge of the circular cake.

Prizes and favors

★ Doll clothes, doll jewelry, books of paper dolls, doll-sized baby bottles filled with candy.

Chapter

31

Slumber Party (Ages 5-10)

I've hosted slumber parties for my daughter as she was growing up, and I have to say this: Anyone who decides to host a slumber party is either an insomniac, a serious night person, or a little bit nuts! Of all the parties included in this book, I must say—without a doubt—this is my least favorite.

However, if you're one of those brave souls who thinks it's really fun to be up all night with a bunch of hyper kids, this is the perfect party for you!

Invitations

☆ Purchase inexpensive dolls from an everything-for-a-dollar store and insert them into homemade "sleeping bags," along with the party invitations. Mail in padded envelopes.

(The sleeping bags can be as simple as narrow brown envelopes or quilted fabric sewn on your sewing machine.) In the invitation, ask the children to bring their sleeping bags, pillows, pajamas, robes, big fuzzy slippers, and a stuffed animal to the party (preferably one who likes to sleep all night).

Attire

✮ Playclothes for the rowdy activities and pajamas, of course, for the sleepover!

Decorations

✮ You can't possibly improve on the natural ambiance of a sleepover scene, with all the colorful sleeping bags, pajamas, slippers, and stuffed animals.

Amusements

✮ I highly recommend planning an exhausting activity early in the evening to wear the children out! You can have relay races in the backyard, a jump-rope contest, volleyball, or anything else you can think of—the rowdier, the better.

✮ Have a pillow fight. (You might want to play this game outside on the lawn.) The children pair up and go piggyback, one playing the horse and the other the rider. The object is for a rider to use a pillow to knock as many other riders as possible off their horses. The last rider left on horseback wins.

✮ Consider wearing them out with an away activity, such as roller skating, ice skating, swimming, or sledding.

✮ Stage a pajama fashion show, using silly nightshirts and big fuzzy slippers.

✮ Videotape the evening's activities and show the tape before (the ever elusive) bedtime.

✮ Speaking of bedtime, once you've exhausted the children as much as you can and served the refreshments, snuggle them down into their sleeping bags in front of the TV and let them watch as many rented movies as it takes for them to get sleepy (hah!). Recommended movies: *The Princess Bride, Home Alone, The Little Mermaid.*

Edibles

★ A slumber party requires lots of eats: a light supper and the birthday cake before or after the rowdy activities, followed by plenty of non-sugary snacks during the movies, such as popcorn, pretzels, and chips and dip. Make sure the drinks you serve are caffeine-free.

★ After such a good night's sleep (!), you'll be in a great mood to fix a hearty breakfast: juice, sausage, pancakes, and the all-time slumber party favorite—hot chocolate with mini-marshmallows and whipped cream.

    Note: An easy alternative to pancakes are Do-it-Yourself Waffles (see Chapter 73).

Prizes and favors

★ Everything-for-a-dollar store dolls, silly nightshirts or T-shirts, comic books, costume jewelry, makeup kits, instant photos.

Tip

★ I'll pray for you!

Winter Wonderland Party (Ages 5-10)

snow party involves outdoor fun in the snow, followed by a warm, cozy indoor party. The object is to allow enough time for outdoor activities, but not so much that the children are shivering from the cold.

Invitations

☆ Attach invitations to small sleigh Christmas tree ornaments (available at your year-round Christmas store). Be sure to specify that the children need to bring warm, waterproof outdoor clothing.

Decorations

✮   Make a snowman centerpiece out of Styrofoam balls. Tie
     a bright "scarf" around his neck, top him with a black top
     hat fashioned from black construction paper, and draw a
     face with felt tip markers. Set the snowman on a blanket of
     snow (a roll of cotton).

Amusements

✮   Do the usual fun outdoor snow activities: Ice skate at a
     neighborhood pond, go snow-sledding or tubing, build a
     snowman, and make angels in the snow. Be sure to provide
     plenty of props for decorating the snowman: hats, car-
     rots, silk flowers, scarves, sunglasses, shawls, jewelry, rai-
     sins, radishes, and so on.

✮   Make snowflakes—This is an indoor activity. Provide the
     children with white squares of paper that have been folded
     into quarters, along with scissors. Have the children cut pat-
     terns in the folded edges so that, when opened, they will
     have a snowflake. (Before they begin, illustrate by cut-
     ting out a beautiful snowflake before their very eyes!)

✮   Gather buckets of clean snow to make Snow Ice Cream.

✮   If the outdoor activities are cut short due to severe weather,
     choose one or two of the games from Chapter 4.

Edibles

✮   Pineapple Boat Kebobs and Bean Boats (see Chapter 72).

✮   Frost a round birthday cake with white frosting. At the
     last minute, cover the top of the cake with "snowballs" (scoops
     of vanilla ice cream rolled in coconut).

✮   Snow Ice Cream (see Chapter 73).

✮   Hot chocolate with "snow" (whipped cream) and "snow-
     balls" (mini-marshmallows).

Prizes and favors

✮   Snowman decorating props, mittens, scarves, coloring books, sticker
     books, instant photos.

Chapter

33

One-Eyed Pirate Party (Ages 6-10)

A One-Eyed Pirate Party is a popular theme because children enjoy pretending they are pirates.

Invitations

☆ Make one black eye patch to enclose with each invitation (attach black elastic to round pieces of black felt or poster board). Ask the children to wear their eye patches, along with pirate outfits—ragged shorts, bright, striped shirts, and bandanas tied around their foreheads. Note: Black pirate eye patches are also available through U.S. Toys catalog (see Resources).

Attire

☆ When the guests arrive, use an eyebrow pencil to draw bushy eyebrows and facial scars.

☆ You should be dressed as the fiercest, scariest pirate of them all. The kids will love it as you greet them at the door!

Decorations

☆ Hang floor-length streamers of black crepe paper in the front entryway.

☆ Provide a pirate's sword for each child as a party favor. Purchase them at a party supply store or at an anything-for-a-dollar store, or make them from heavy cardboard, spray-painted gold. Cover the handle with glued-on pieces of old costume jewelry or brightly colored jewel-like buttons.

☆ Decorate with homemade skull-and-crossbones flags or posters, made from black and white fabric or poster board.

☆ Draw a pirate's map on an 8 1/2" x 11" piece of paper. Make copies to serve as placemats.

☆ Set black and silver helium balloons in clusters of three on the serving table, as well as around the room.

☆ Make a treasure chest centerpiece from a shoebox by spray-painting it with silver paint and embellishing with foil and jewels (buttons or pieces from old costume jewelry). Fill the box with gold coin candies, and leave the lid open so they're visible.

☆ Use pieces of plywood or large cardboard appliance boxes to build a pirate ship. If the party will be held outdoors, use a swing set as its foundation. If indoors, convert an assembly of chairs and other furniture into a ship. Be sure to fly the skull and crossbones flag from the ship's mast!

Amusements

☆ Gather the children in a circle on the floor as you read (or tell) them a scary pirate story. Visit the children's section of your local library for ideas.

★ Have a treasure hunt: Create a treasure map that leads the children from one clue to another throughout the yard until they finally come to the X that marks the spot of the buried treasure (a coffee can filled with jelly beans or gold coin candies). Optional: You can divide the children up into teams. Sample clues:

1. Start at the back of the doghouse.

2. Take 10 steps forward until you see a red ribbon on the fence.

3. Follow a path that leads to a big rock. Look under the rock.

4. Take 20 hops backward until you come to a silver shed. Look inside, where you'll find a tall shovel.

5. Attached to the top of the shovel is a map that leads to the X marking the buried treasure.

★ If your pirates have energy to spare, calm them down with a video, such as *Peter Pan* or *Hook.*

Edibles

★ Serve pirate's fare: Cups of "blood" (cold tomato juice), a bucket filled with Long John Silver's rum (apple juice), barbecued chicken or turkey legs, potatoes "roasted" in the fire (pre-cooked whole potatoes with their skins on), bananas, and sliced pineapple.

★ Provide "pirates' daggers" (forks with a swatch of a red bandana tied to the handle) to use as utensils.

★ Serve Hidden Treasure Birthday Cupcakes. Bake ordinary cupcakes, and after cupcakes have cooled, press jelly beans or any type of candy inside each cupcake. Add frosting, and top with lighted candles to be blown out by the birthday child.

Prizes and favors

★ Bandanas, pirate swords, eye patches.

Wild West Party (Ages 6-11)

C hildren enjoy dressing up as cowboys, pioneers, sheriffs, Indians, and Wild West characters such as Daniel Boone or Davy Crockett. Although this can be an indoor party, or held in the garage or on the patio, it works best outdoors around a campfire.

Invitations

☆ Attach the invitations to miniature cowboy hats, which can be purchased at party supply stores. Ask the guests to come dressed as Wild West characters, such as cowboys or frontiersmen, wearing boots, plaid flannel shirts, cowboy or coonskin hats, fringed leather jackets, and so forth.

Decorations

☆ Give each guest a red bandana for his neck or a toy star badge for his chest.
☆ Create a Wild West campsite, with Indian teepees (made from poles and brown butcher paper or burlap fabric), a campfire,

bales of hay as chairs, cast iron frying pans, blue enamel camping cups, bedrolls, real or cardboard cactuses, a saddle, and pairs of cowboy boots.

Amusements

* ✮ Gather around the campfire and tell scary or exciting Wild West stories (visit the children's section of your library for ideas).
* ✮ Provide the materials for the children to make their own bows and arrows: 3' lengths of bendable tree branches, string, sturdy plastic straws, tape, and cotton balls. Help the children make notches at the ends of each of the branches to secure the bowstrings. Use straws as arrows, but tape cotton balls to the ends to prevent eye injuries.
* ✮ Sing cowboy songs, such as Home on the Range and Don't Fence Me In.
* ✮ Provide each child with a water pistol. Line up a row of lighted candles about 20 feet away from the children and have a shootout. Give a prize to the child who shoots out the most candle flames with three tries.
* ✮ Play Musical Saddles, using camp stools or bales of hay as chairs. This is played the same way as Musical Chairs (see Chapter 4), but with country-western music.
* ✮ Have a roping contest. Make a lasso by tying a slip knot in a piece of rope and taking turns trying to lasso the horns of a bull—that is, the handle-bars of a bicycle.
* ✮ Have horse or pony rides.
* ✮ Take each child's instant photo (furnish a cowboy hat and bandana for the photo op). Frame the photos in Wanted posters you have made ahead of time. Fill in their names on the posters and send them home with the children as party favors.

Edibles

* ✮ Let the kids roast their own hot dogs over the fire. Top them with chili and serve on pieces of French bread.
* ✮ Provide camping mess kits as dishes, metal cups as glasses, and a couple of blue enamelware coffeepots as pitchers.
* ✮ Serve a Character Bundt Cake (see Chapter 73) with a cowboy inserted into the hole in the center of the cake.

Prizes and favors

* ✮ Toy cowboys or Indians, water pistols, cowboy hats, bandanas, lassos, instant photo "wanted" posters, and the bows and arrows they made during the party.

Camp-Over Party (Ages 7-10)

This party is an overnight sleepover that takes place outdoors in tents. You can go from a backyard sleepover, to a camp-out in nearby woods, to a destination trip to state or national campgrounds.

Invitations

☆ Fold a piece of 5 1/2" x 11" brown construction paper into the shape of a tent. Place the paper lengthwise and fold down the upper right and left corners, forming front flaps for the tent. Use black felt-tip pen to print the invitation on the inside of the tent (so that it can be seen when the flaps are lifted). Enclose in an oversized envelope and mail. Include a suggested list of gear, including sleeping bags, pillows, blankets, flashlights, daypacks, hiking boots or tennis shoes, hats, long-sleeved shirts, and long pants.

Attire

☆ Wear appropriate camping clothes, depending on the weather.

Decorations

★ By the time you set up the tents and build a camp fire, you won't need any other decorations.

Amusements

★ Go on a bug hike. Load the kids' daypacks with canned juices and snacks and take them on a bug hike. Provide one bug catcher per child (can be purchased at a toy store or homemade by punching holes in the lids of glass jars).

★ Have a nature scavenger hunt. (See Chapter 37 for ideas.)

★ Let the children help put up the tents and lay out their sleeping bags. This will be pretty exciting for the kids, especially those who haven't camped out before.

★ Have a sack race with the kids inside their sleeping bags (see Chapter 3).

★ After dinner, play Flashlight Tag or Black Wolf (see Chapter 3)—both are great games to play outdoors in the wilderness after dark.

★ After the games, let the children roast popcorn over the fire (see Chapter 71).

Edibles

★ Trail mix, Cracker Jacks, and canned juice before dinner.

★ Serve Wilderness Stew (canned stew heated over the fire) and Wilderness Hot Dogs (let the kids roast their own). Roast marshmallows after dinner, which can be eaten whole or used to make s'mores (see Chapter 73), along with the birthday cake, of course. (Decorate a round cake with a miniature brown construction paper tent and a campfire, made out of tiny twigs).

★ For breakfast, fry bacon over the fire and make Happy Face Pancakes (small pancakes with eyes and mouth made with chocolate syrup).

Prizes and favors

★ Bug catchers, mini-flashlights, compasses, magnifying glasses.

Tips

★ If you don't have a supply of tents, you can improvise by hanging a rug, bedspread or blanket over a clothesline or picnic table. (Use a plastic tarp to cover the ground.)

★ If inclement weather is forecast for the day of the party, move it indoors. Set up the tents in the basement or the garage, and use your charcoal barbecue outdoors for the cooking.

Chapter

36

Whodunnit Party (Ages 8-12)

This party theme gives the children a chance to try to figure out "who done it," as they pretend they are detectives.

Invitations

☆ Use narrow ribbon to tie the invitations to small magnifying glasses. Mail them in padded envelopes. Ask the children to come dressed as detectives and to bring the magnifying glasses with them to the party.

Note: You can buy small magnifying glasses from the U.S. Toys catalog (see Resources) or you can make facsimiles from lightweight poster board.

Attire

★ Greet the children at the door wearing a trench coat, dark sunglasses, and a hat pulled down over your eyes. Jokingly examine each child with a large magnifying glass before you allow him or her to enter.

Decorations

★ In the middle of your main party room, lay a large stuffed animal on the floor and cover it with a sheet, to make it resemble a murder victim.

★ Tape oversized mock newspaper headlines to the walls, such as "Unsolved Mystery on [name of your street]" or "Police Have Suspect in Murder Case." Hand print or computer generate the headlines, or use actual newspaper headlines you have enlarged on your scanner or on a photocopy machine. Use newspaper photos, too, if any appropriate ones are available.

★ Suspend toy water pistols from the ceiling using string, fishing line, or pieces of dental floss.

★ Set a dozen or so "suspects" (dolls, stuffed animals, or monster figures, depending on the ages of your guests) in a "line-up."

Amusements

★ Play "Whodunnit?": Explain to the children that one of the suspects in the line-up committed the murder. Send the children out on the case to gather clues. Write the clues on 3 x 5 cards and hide them around the house or yard. Create clues that relate to your murderer. For example, if the teddy bear did it, here are a few suggested clues:

1. The footprints leading away from the crime scene showed that the murderer was barefoot.

2. A witness said she saw someone short and dark running away from the house after the murder.

3. Police discovered brown hair or fur stuck to the front gate.

4. Police reports show that the victim was hugged to death.

☆ For older children, play "Whodunnit?" by dividing the children into teams of three or four, naming several famous movie or TV characters as suspects, and allowing each team to secretly pick one of the characters as the murderer. Each team writes its own clues about that character and gets a turn reading the clues aloud to all of the other teams. The children from the other teams have to guess which character is being described. The first child in each group who guesses a team's character is a winner.

☆ Play a round of the Clue board game.

☆ Challenge the children to a game of Super Sleuth. Assemble them in a circle, and ask each child to draw a piece of paper from a hat. One of the pieces of paper should be marked with an X. The others should be blank. The child who draws the X is the murderer and kills his or her victims by winking at them. When a player sees that he or she is being winked at, that player should play-act dying as dramatically as possible, falling into the center of the circle. The object of the game is for the rest of the players to try to figure out who the murderer is before they are "killed." The game ends when the murderer has finally "killed" every-one, or when someone correctly identifies the murderer. (The game may be repeated by drawing from the hat again.)

☆ Show a mystery movie rented from your video store.

Edibles

☆ Serve movie food, such as hot dogs, chips, popcorn, and soda.

☆ Decorate the birthday cake with an actual magnifying glass and the words, "It's No Mystery That We Wish [name of birthday child] a Happy Birthday!"

Prizes and favors

☆ Magnifying glass, dark sunglasses, water pistols.

Chapter

37

Super Scavenger Hunt (Ages 8-12)

A scavenger hunt is a popular theme for children in this age bracket, whether it involves going door-to-door, searching in the yard, or scavenging inside your home.

Invitations

★ Attach small flashlights to each invitation (to help during the scavenger hunt). Ask the children to bring their flashlights with them to the party.

Attire

★ If the party is held outdoors, guests should dress appropriately for the weather.

Decorations

☆ No special decorations required for this party, other than normal birth-day decor—balloons, streamers, party hats, etc.

Amusements

☆ Scavenger Hunt—Of course, the scavenger hunt is the theme of this party, so it needs to be a good one. There are several ways to orchestrate a scavenger hunt, depending on the weather and where you live:

1. **Outdoor Scavenger Hunt**—This is similar to an Easter egg hunt, only the children are looking for specific items you have hidden in the yard ahead of time. For example, you can hide a large supply of wrapped candies, nickels wrapped in foil, and small party favors, such as wrapped bubble bath or toy cars (depend-ing on the guests). Send the children on their hunt with instruc-tions to bring back only one of each item.

    Tip: For younger children, hide the items in places that are easy for them to spot—for example, on a section of a tree limb at about their eye level. For older children, you can make the hunt more of a challenge by hiding items under the sand in the sandbox, inside a sack of dog food, or under the lid of the barbe-cue grill, for example.

2. **Indoor Scavenger Hunt**—Hopefully, the weather will allow you to have the Hunt outdoors. If not, just play it indoors.

3. **Door-to-Door Scavenger Hunt**—This is the traditional form of a scavenger hunt, where each child is given a list of items he must retrieve by knocking on doors in the neighborhood. It works best to have items that don't need to be returned to the neigh-bors. You can make up your own list of items, or you can bor-row ideas from this list:

    • Piece of chewing gum.
    • Empty tin can.
    • Plastic spoon.
    • Band-Aid adhesive bandage.
    • Rubber band.
    • Key chain.
    • One glove.

- Golf ball.
- Piece of foil.
- Spool of thread.
- One sock.
- Day-old newspaper.
- Popsicle stick.
- One nail.
- Roll of toilet paper.
- One red paper plate.
- One candle.
- Toothpick.
- Clothespin.
- Refrigerator magnet.
- Magazine.
- Cookie.
- One drinking straw.
- Peanut butter and jelly sandwich.
- One penny.
- Red pencil.

Edibles

☆ Serve Jell-O Jigglers, mini-pizza and Rocky Road Sandwiches (see Chapters 72 and 73), along with a birthday cake decorated with a real magnifying glass.

Prizes and favors

☆ Magnifying glasses, mini-flashlights, compasses.

Tips

☆ You can simplify a scavenger hunt by calling it a nature hunt. Ask the children to retrieve things that can be found in nature around your house, such as an acorn, tree moss, a pine cone, and so on.

☆ If the hunt takes place door to door, you'll need several adults to help supervise and keep the children safe, especially when crossing streets.

Chapter
38

San Francisco Party (Ages 8-12)

This is a novelty spaghetti dinner party older kids will love. As you know, San Francisco is known for its steep hills, so the idea is to set the table with tall containers from your kitchen, which are covered with a sheet, forming the San Francisco peaks.

Invitations

⭐ Hand-print the wording on the backs of post cards or photos of the San Francisco skyline. Let the guests know it is to be a dinner and that they should wear their "grubbies" to the party, but keep the rest a surprise.

Decorations

⭐ Raid your kitchen for tall pots, pans, pitchers, mixing bowls, colanders, or storage containers, which will serve as plates and salad bowls.

☆ Canning jars, empty salt and pepper shakers, gravy boats, measuring cups, etc. serve as glasses.

☆ Spatulas, soup ladles, measuring cup and ice cream scoops serve as utensils. Set each place at the table, using items described above. When all the places are set, cover the entire table with white sheets, which will create hills and peaks.

☆ When the children arrive, they each choose a place and sit down at the table, but they can't peek to see what's under the sheets. When all the children have arrived and are seated, the sheets are removed and the meal is served.

☆ The "mounded" table will be the center of attention, of course, but you can also add travel posters for San Francisco (visit your friendly travel agent).

Amusements

☆ The meal will be very entertaining, believe me, or you can add:

☆ "Street Entertainers"—as you may know, San Francisco, especially the Fisherman's Wharf area, is known for its street entertainers. Hire an amateur or professional juggler, balloon artist, face painter, puppeteer, caricaturist, magician, one-man band, tap dancer, or novelty act to entertain the children after they've eaten.

Edibles

☆ The meal consists of spaghetti, salad, garlic bread, and soda or lemonade. The dessert (from Chapter 73) can include a birthday cake decorated with a mini-Golden Gate Bridge and peaks of frosting in the background.

The spaghetti is served on the children's "plates" (cooking pots, etc.), the salad is placed in the "salad bowls" (colanders, etc.) and the drinks are poured into their "glasses" (gravy boat, etc.) Then, the fun begins as they eat the meal using only their "utensils" (spatulas, soup ladles, and so on).

The dessert, whether a birthday cake or another choice, may also be served on novelty dishes with novelty utensils, or you can use paper plates and plastic tableware.

Prizes and favors

☆ San Francisco skyline puzzles or travel posters, yo-yos, kazoos, face paint, instant photos.

Chapter

39

Aloha Party (Ages 8-12)

An Aloha Party, also called a Polynesian Party or luau, is a popular idea for this age group. The Hawaiian party theme plans itself and becomes one of the most carefree, least stressful birthday parties you'll ever put together.

Invitations

☆   Attach hand-printed or computer-generated invitations to silk or synthetic leis and mail to each guest. Ask the guests to wear their leis to the party, along with Hawaiian attire.

Attire

☆   Grass skirts and halter tops.

☆   Hawaiian shirts/sarongs/muumuus.

116

* ☆ Colorful leis, beads or shell necklaces.
* ☆ Flowers in the girls' hair.
* ☆ Bare feet.

  Tip: If it's wintertime, turn the thermostat to 80 degrees and pretend you're in the tropics.

Decorations

* ☆ Hawaiian brochures and travel posters.
* ☆ Hang fishnets from the ceilings and over doorways. Fill the fishnets with fish-shaped balloons or plastic fish.
* ☆ Set plants and large, colorful fresh or silk flowers around the room or patio.
* ☆ Use large palm fronds or grass mats as place mats, or to cover the serving table.
* ☆ If you have a pool, float a rubber raft filled with colorful flowers.
* ☆ Use colorful beach towels to decorate the party site.
* ☆ Use a fish bowl with live goldfish as the table centerpiece.
* ☆ Place a fresh or silk flower, or a tiny paper parasol, in the center of each place setting, or stick the flower or parasol into the top of a straw that is placed in the beverage glass.

Amusements

* ☆ Play Hawaiian background music throughout the party.
* ☆ If the party takes place around a pool, include swimming as an activity.
* ☆ Make edible headbands. Let the children sew wrapped candies together, using long strands of dental floss cut into headband lengths, threaded through large, blunt needles, with three or four inches left over for tying together. Tie a piece of curled crinkle ribbon at each juncture of candy, hiding the dental floss and decorating the headband. The children may wear their headbands, which become party favors when they leave the party.
* ☆ Have a hula contest. Purchase inexpensive hula skirts from your favorite import store or make them with strips of green crepe paper or

plastic garbage bags (which can be tucked into waistbands). Tie skirts around a few of the guests, play recorded Hawaiian music, and see how well they can hula.

☆ Hula lessons, whether amateur or professional, are always popular.

☆ Have a hula hoop contest—an interesting twist to the party.

☆ Videotape the activities and show the tape near the end of the party.

Edibles

☆ Option 1: Mini Hawaiian Luau
  - Roasted bananas (peel, dip in melted butter, and sprinkle with sugar; wrap in aluminum foil and roast for 20 minutes).
  - Hawaiian Fruit Kabobs (chunks of fresh fruit, such as pineapple, melon, bananas, oranges, and grapes, placed on wooden skewers).
  - Sweet Hawaiian bread.
  - A bowl of poi (of course)! Poi is taro root paste. Kids love to make faces and say how gross it is!
  - Polynesian smoothies (see Chapter 74).

☆ Option 2 – Cake and ice cream (frame the cake with a fresh flower lei).
  - Polynesian Lei Cake: Set cupcakes in a circle, connected with red licorice vines. Add fresh or silk leaves on the sides of the cupcakes. Decorate the cupcakes with frosting and candy flowers. Use frosting to write one letter on each cupcake, spelling out "Happy Birthday [child's name]."
  - Hawaiian Volcano Punch: Fill a punch bowl with fruit punch and scoops of raspberry sherbet. Pour cold raspberry soda or ginger ale over the sherbet, which will foam, creating a volcano effect.

Prizes and favors

☆ Silk or synthetic leis, beads, shell necklaces, tiny paper parasols, edible headbands, candy leis, hula hoops, instant photos.

Tip

☆ Dress the part, hang loose, and enjoy the party from beginning to end!

Birthday Parties for Teens

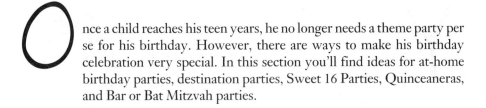

Once a child reaches his teen years, he no longer needs a theme party per se for his birthday. However, there are ways to make his birthday celebration very special. In this section you'll find ideas for at-home birthday parties, destination parties, Sweet 16 Parties, Quinceaneras, and Bar or Bat Mitzvah parties.

Chapter
40

At-Home Birthday Parties for Teens

Y ou have several options for this type of party, depending on the preferences of your teen. Your daughter may want to have her girlfriends over to swim in your pool, play video games, watch rented movies, or have a sleepover. She'll probably appreciate a couple of balloon bouquets, a decorated serving table, and a personalized birthday cake.

Your son, however, will probably prefer a destination party so he can get away with his male friends. If you decide to plan an at-home party for him, be sure you talk it over with him first so you know what's in and what's out. For example, balloons, streamers, and a cutesy birthday cake are definitely out for male teen parties. (In fact, they would probably embarrass your son to death!) What's in? Unchaperoned activities, such as swimming, volleyball, video games, darts, or rented movies. As for decorations, cover your table with plenty of eats!

Coed parties are more appropriate for older teens. You can include most of the activities mentioned above, plus they may enjoy dancing, especially if you have a decent dance floor and sound system. If the teens are old enough to drive, they may also enjoy one of the parties described in Part 7—Just-for-the-Fun-of-It Parties—such as a Video Scavenger Hunt or Tailgate Party.

For a coed party, decorate according to the theme, or give it a light or heavy touch, depending on whether it is your son's or daughter's birthday.

Edibles

Teen parties require *lots* of food, such these teen favorites:

☆ Pizza.

☆ Hamburgers.

☆ Chili.

☆ Spaghetti.

☆ Hot garlic bread.

☆ Lasagna.

☆ Make-your-own tacos and burritos.

☆ Bean boats (see Chapter 72).

☆ Hero sandwiches (see Chapter 72).

☆ Chips, dips and other snack foods.

☆ Plenty of cold soda.

☆ Ice cream sundaes and banana splits.

Chapter
____
41

Destination Parties for Teens

Adestination party is easier to plan than an at-home party. You can't go wrong if you plan a destination birthday party for your teenager, as long as your child is in on the plans and approves of the destination.

Here are a few favorites:

☆   Water skiing.

☆   A day at the beach.

☆   White water rafting or tubing.

☆   Miniature golf.

☆   Hay ride or sleigh ride.

☆   Partying at a rented summer camp facility after camp season is over.

☆   Cross country or downhill skiing.

☆   Attending a favorite movie, followed by a trip to a pizza parlor.

☆   Tailgate party before a professional football, basketball, or hockey game (see Chapter 62).

☆   Live theater or concert performance.

☆   An afternoon at a family fun center or amusement park.

☆   Ice-skating or roller-skating.

☆   Trip to a famous tourist attraction—for example, a ferry ride to the Statue of Liberty if you live near New York City, or lunch at the top of the Space Needle if you live near Seattle.

☆   Partying on a houseboat for a day, with swimming and a barbecue.

Attire

☆   Be specific about the activities involved so that the teens can dress accordingly.

Decorations

☆   Ask your teenager whether he or she would like a few balloons and a birthday cake at the destination site—many teens (especially older ones) prefer not to call attention to themselves in public.

Edibles

☆   The food will be easy to plan once you've decided on a destination. For example, if you'll be cross country skiing, plan a campfire and barbecue at the end of the trail, or combine mini-golf with a trip to a nearby pizza parlor.

Tip

☆   Involve your teen in the plans. If he doesn't have ideas of his own, sit down together and look through the yellow pages for destination party sites.

Chapter

42

Quinceañera

A Quinceañera, pronounced "keen-see-an-yeah-ra," is a significant and memorable event that celebrates a Latina girl's passage into womanhood and her debut into society. It usually takes place on her 15th birthday, although many families, including those in the northeastern United States, often wait a year and call it a Sweet Sixteen. This lavish celebration is a significant event for the girl and her relatives, often requiring 18 months to two years of preparation. It is taken very seriously and observed by families of varied financial means.

A Quinceañera celebration is usually, but not always, preceded by a church service. This service is considered an important element of the

Quinceañera and often includes scripture readings, the renewal of baptismal vows, a prayer of thanksgiving, presentation of 15 red roses to the girl by her family and the blessing and presentation of gifts to the girl by her family and sponsors.

The Quinceañera reception usually includes a formal ball that is choreographed from beginning to end as follows:

- ✩ Presentation of the Quinceañera in a formal entrance ceremony.
- ✩ First dance with her father (during which, according to tradition, she passes into womanhood).
- ✩ First dance with her escort.
- ✩ Public speech of thanks by the Quinceañera to her family.
- ✩ General dancing, usually including a traditional Quinceañera waltz.

Total costs for this Cinderella day can run anywhere from $1,000 to more than $100,000, which is why sponsors, known as padrinos, often contribute financially to the celebration. Padrinos are friends and family members who not only help out with the costs, but agree to fulfill one or more of the many responsibilities involved with the planning. Here are just a few of the costs a sponsor may agree to pay for:

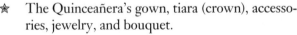

- ✩ The Quinceañera's gown, tiara (crown), accessories, jewelry, and bouquet.
- ✩ Professional choreographer (to incorporate a theme and plan the presentation of the Quinceañera at her entrance ceremony).
- ✩ Cushions for the Quinceañera to kneel upon.
- ✩ Photographer and videographer, including formal portrait.
- ✩ Invitations to the prospective members of the Quinceañera's court (often 15 girls and 15 boys), invitations to the celebration; reception and reply cards, pew cards, thank-you scrolls and thank-you notes, place cards, programs, and menu cards.
- ✩ Transportation services, often including a limousine or carriage.
- ✩ Musical entertainment, including a mariachi to play at the church and/ or reception.
- ✩ Reception site, including food and drink (which are always lavish and abundant).
- ✩ Exquisitely decorated multi-tiered cake (with gazebo, fountains, and dolls that represent the Quinceañera and the girls in her court).

☆ Decorations and flowers for the home, church, and reception site.

☆ The Capia Doll and Last Doll.

☆ Ceramic souvenirs to be given to the guests.

☆ Gold ring.

☆ Toasting glasses for the Quinceañera, her escort, members of her court, and her sponsors.

☆ Prayer book, Bible, or rosary.

☆ Possible rental of tables, tents, chairs, portable dance floor, wicker floral baskets, decorated arch, and candelabra.

Tips

☆ In lieu of the traditional celebration, many Quinceañeras opt for a gift, often a trip abroad, a cruise, or a new car. As a matter of fact, some cruise lines, such as Carnival Fun Ships, cater to the Quinceañera and her family by offering a party that includes a debutante ball, a candlelight ceremony, and the traditional Quinceañera waltz.

☆ A traditional Quinceañera celebration can be more complex, elaborate, and expensive than the average wedding. Therefore, it should come as no surprise that entire books have been written on the subject. This is my personal favorite:

Quinceañera; The Essential Guide to Planning the Perfect Sweet Fifteen Celebration, by Michele Salcedo.

Chapter

43

Sweet 16 Parties

When a girl reaches her 16th birthday, she may be honored with a special celebration called a Sweet 16. Turning 16 is considered by many to be a milestone signifying the division between childhood and adulthood. The party is usually hosted by the girl's parents, grandparents, or aunt and uncle.

This party can be an all-girl party, which many girls prefer, or one to which boys are invited. Often the party is a dressy affair that includes dinner and dancing, with a live band or a DJ. Other options include a destination party (see Chapter 41) or a special night out to a concert, theater performance, or an exhibition ice-skating show. Offer your daughter several options—the choice is up to her.

Invitations

☆ A formal party, such as a dinner dance, calls for formal invitations. For a coed party, you can invite the guests to bring dates.

☆ An informal, at-home party, such as a sleepover (see Chapter 31 for ideas), gives your daughter the option of extending invitations by word of mouth or over the telephone.

Attire

☆ A dinner dance requires formal or semiformal attire.

☆ A sleepover requires pajamas, robes, and slippers.

☆ Guests should dress appropriately for a novelty party—for example, a party that includes a hayride or, on the opposite side of the spectrum, a theater performance.

Decorations

☆ If this is to be a formal dinner dance, it may be held in a hotel ballroom, at a country club or in a hall, in which case more elaborate decorations will be required.

☆ Wherever the party is held, you can create a table centerpiece with an arrangement of 16 candles in candleholders of various heights. Tie narrow satin ribbons around the bases of the candles.

Amusements

☆ A dinner dance or special event will provide its own entertainment.

☆ For an informal party's entertainment, have a makeup consultant do makeovers for the girls.

☆ Gift opening is a big part of any Sweet 16 party.

Edibles

☆ Pizza, salad, and French bread are hits at sleepovers. Top them off with a special dessert, such as Make-Your-Own Sundaes (see Chapter 73).

☆ A late night supper or light dessert buffet may be served at home after attending a special event.

☆ Be sure to include a few of the birthday girl's favorite dishes.

☆ A birthday cake is a must, complete with 16 candles, of course!

Chapter
44

Bar or Bat Mitzvah Parties

hen Jewish boys and girls turn 13 (sometimes 12 for girls), their coming of age is marked with a celebration to observe the Bar Mitzvah (son of the commandment) or Bat Mitzvah (daughter of the commandment). The religious ceremony is typically held at a Saturday morning (Sabbath) service in which a portion of the Torah is recited. Most families follow the ceremony with a party of some sort. The party may be anything from a casual luncheon with no theme at all to a novelty destination affair, such as a riverboat cruise, to an all-out formal dinner dance with no expense spared.

In addition to the Saturday morning service and party later that day, it is quite common to involve an entire weekend, from Friday evening through Sunday brunch.

Invitations

☆　Formal parties require formal invitations.

129

Invitations for informal parties may be extended by word of mouth or with store-bought invitations.

Attire

☆ From casual to black tie, depending on the formality of the scheduled events.

Decorations

☆ Although it is not imperative to have a theme, it has become popular to honor the Bar or Bat Mitzvah child with a theme related to one of the child's interests or talents. For example, if she is the star of her soccer team, you can decorate with soccer balls, soccer nets, large posters created from photos of her in her soccer uniform, and so forth.

Amusements

☆ Choose a gift for each individual child in attendance, matching the gift to each child's special interest or hobby.

☆ Hire a band or small group of musicians to entertain, especially if you plan to host a formal dinner dance.

☆ If the festivities span the weekend, you may want to plan a few physical activities, such as skating, hiking, swimming, or bowling.

Edibles

☆ If the festivities extend from Friday evening through Sunday brunch, you'll need to plan several menus. If you're having a large, sit-down luncheon or a formal dinner, you may prefer to hire a caterer. That way you'll feel more relaxed and be able to enjoy your guests.

Tips

☆ Why not splurge and hire a limousine and driver to transport the honored child and his guests to and from the scheduled events?

☆ Prepare a gift basket for each out-of-town guest. Deliver the baskets to the guests' hotel to be placed in their rooms, or place them in the guest bedroom in your home or that of nearby relatives.

Part

4

Seasonal Parties

W hether you're planning a special seasonal party for your child's class at school or you want to host an at home party over the holidays, this section includes six popular seasonal parties for kids, complete with party games, activities, and menu suggestions.

Chapter

45

Valentine's Day Party

Valentine's Day, February 14, is a holiday favorite for children. You'll find the ideas in this chapter adaptable to a large class party or a smaller party at home.

Invitations

✯   Purchase a box of children's valentines to use as party invitations. Attach one valentine to each invitation, or print the invitation on the back of each.

Attire

✯   Encourage the kids to wear red or pink.

Decorations

✯   Decorate with large red, white, and pink hearts cut from construction paper and embellished with red ribbons and white paper lace.

✯ Invert a colander and fill with red, heart-shaped lollipops inserted into the holes. Tie each lollipop at its neck with a red ribbon.

✯ Set small, red, heart-shaped boxes of chocolates in the center of each place setting as party favors.

✯ Place clusters of heart-shaped balloons around the room, on the serving table, or tied in groups of three to the backs of chairs.

✯ Add red, white, and pink crepe paper streamers to the lamppost in the front yard, the entryway and doorways.

✯ Sprinkle the table with metallic, heart-shaped confetti, available from your party supply store or through Anderson's Prom and Party Catalog (see Resources).

✯ Hang a Valentine's Day mural on the wall, also available through Anderson's.

Amusements

✯ Have the children guess how many candy hearts are in a glass jar or fish bowl. The winner gets to keep the container of candy hearts as a prize.

✯ Give each child one unfinished wooden heart (available from craft and hobby stores) along with acrylic craft paints and permanent markers. Let them decorate their hearts to take home as party favors.

✯ Spoon Race (see Chapter 4)—Use spoons to pass small candy hearts. The winning team receives a heart-shaped box of Valentine chocolates.

✯ Bake and decorate Valentine's cookies—Purchase ready-to-use sugar cookie dough. Let the kids roll out the dough, cut into heart shapes, bake in the oven, and then decorate with pink frosting and hot red cinnamon candies or sprinkles.

Edibles

✯ Make-Your-Own Fruit Kabobs—Prepare wooden skewers and chunks of fresh fruit (grapes, melons, bananas, strawberries, pineapple, peaches, etc.) and let the children assemble their own kabobs.

✯ Decorated heart-shaped cookies or a heart-shaped cake.

✯ Red, bubbly Valentine's Day punch—fill a punch bowl with cold fruit punch, raspberry sherbet and cold raspberry soda. (The punch will foam and bubble when the carbonated soda is poured over the sherbet.)

St. Patrick's Day Party

March 17 is St. Patrick's Day, a day that honors the saint who brought Christianity to Ireland in the 5th century. Here are ideas for a St. Patrick's Day children's party:

Invitations

☆ Cut 8" shamrocks out of heavy green paper and print the invitation on the back, or attach the shamrocks to computer-generated invitations. Request that the children wear something green to the party.

Decorations

☆ Greet your guests at the door with a life size leprechaun, available through Advanced Graphics (see Resources).

* ✯ Talk your travel agent out of a few Irish travel brochures or posters.
* ✯ Provide a "Blarney Stone" for the kids to kiss. (Haul in the biggest rock you can carry from your yard and set it on a bed of crushed green tissue paper.)
* ✯ Think green and white for this party—everything from balloons to crepe paper streamers.
* ✯ Set out "pots of gold" party favors—nut cups filled with gold chocolate coins and covered with gold foil.
* ✯ Decorate with shillelaghs, shamrocks, and clay pipes.

Amusements

* ✯ Give each child a solid-colored hat. It can be any inexpensive, solid-colored hat you can find, such as a straw hat, baseball cap, or a white paper painter's hat (available at your hardware store). Have the children transform their plain hats into green and white St. Patrick's Day hats. Supply them with green crepe paper, St. Patrick's Day stickers, ribbons, buttons, "jewels," shamrocks, and other Irish novelties, along with glue, a stapler, and tape. Award prizes for the funniest, most creative, most beautiful, and so on. Have the children wear their hats during the party and take instant photos they can take home with them as souvenirs.
* ✯ Have the children fish for prizes in a giant "pot-of-gold." Fill a large terra cotta planter with small toys, each with a paper clip attached. Cover the planter with gold foil. Furnish a fishing pole with a magnet attached to the end of the line. Let the children fish for a prize, one child at a time. An adult needs to supervise this fishing expedition so that each child catches only one prize as the magnet retrieves it by attaching to the paper clip.
* ✯ Snake Hunt—This is like an Easter egg hunt (see Chapter 47), except that the children hunt for rubber snakes that have been hidden around the yard or house. (St. Patrick is said to have chased all the snakes out of Ireland.)
* ✯ Play St. Patrick Says instead of Simon Says (see Chapter 4).

Edibles

* ✯ Shamrock Smoothies (see Chapter 74).
* ✯ Shamrock Sugar Cookies: Add three drops of green food coloring to your favorite sugar cookie dough, roll out, cut into shamrock shapes, and top with green sprinkles. You'll find a sugar cookie recipe in Chapter 73.

Chapter

47

Easter Day Party

Easter falls on a Sunday in Spring. Children love traditional Easter festivities, including an Easter egg hunt and egg roll.

Invitations

☆ Attach small, fuzzy, yellow Easter chicks to homemade or store-bought invitations. If it will be a family party, invitations can be made via telephone or e-mail.

Decorations

☆ Decorate your table with pink, yellow, and blue balloons and plastic eggs filled with candy or marshmallow bunnies.

☆ Drape pastel-colored crepe paper streamers across the ceilings and over the front door.

136

☆ Easter egg favors: Hard boil one egg per guest. Decorate the eggs with Easter egg dye, writing the guests' names near the tops of the eggs. Display the eggs in egg cups, tiny baskets filled with Easter basket grass, or homemade egg cups made from egg cartons (cut out each section and spray with gold paint). Place one egg cup or basket at each place setting.

☆ Set tiny decorated Easter baskets filled with candy at each place setting as party favors.

☆ Create a table centerpiece by filling a large Easter basket with plastic grass and stuffed bunnies.

Amusements

☆ If weather permits, play yard games, such as lawn croquet, badminton, or volleyball, depending on the age of the guests.

☆ An Easter egg hunt is a must for the smaller children. Hide decorated hard-boiled eggs, wrapped candies, or marshmallow bunnies around the yard. Provide each child with a basket and send the children on the hunt. (Small children believe, of course, that the treats have been hidden by the Easter Bunny.)

☆ After the small children have finished their Easter egg hunt, hide plastic eggs filled with coins for the older children. Even though they no longer believe in the Easter Bunny, they still enjoy the hunt.

☆ Have an egg decorating contest. Provide hard-boiled eggs, dye, crayons, paper lace, construction paper, felt pieces, glue, and so forth.

☆ Have a traditional egg roll for the children. Poke holes in the ends of raw eggs and blow out the contents of each egg, leaving a light, delicate shell. Reinforce the ends of each egg with colored tape or notebook paper reinforcements. Establish starting and finishing lines about 45 feet apart. Ask the children to get down on their hands and knees at the starting line and blow their eggs to the finish line without blowing so hard the eggs turn end over end. The first child to blow his egg over the finish line without breaking it is declared the winner. You can also have the children roll their eggs with their noses.

☆ Play Pin the Tail on the Rabbit.

☆ Have an Easter bonnet contest for the children. Purchase a supply of plain white paper painters' hats, along with silk flowers, ribbons, and craft supplies for decorations.

✰   Videotape the day's activities; show the tape towards the end of the party.

Edibles

✰   Make-Your-Own Magic Mountains, or

✰   Frozen Fruit Balls, or

✰   Easter Basket Cupcakes, or

✰   Make-Your-Own Sundaes, or

✰   Gummy Worm Cake.

(These dessert recipes can be found in Chapter 73.)

Chapter
48

Halloween Party

Sometimes it's safer—and a lot more fun—to have an at-home Halloween party for the children. It can be a lively, fun, scary, or exciting party that actually results in more take-home treats than they would have had trick-or-treating door to door.

Invitations

★ Cut black poster board into the shape of a bat and write invitations on the back of the bat. Be sure to ask the guests to arrive in costume.

Attire

★ When the children arrive, greet them at the door wearing a mummy costume. (Wrap yourself up from head to toe with gauze bandages or strips of old white sheets. Leave holes for your mouth, nose, and eyes.)

★ The children will be in costume.

Decorations

★ Decorate the yard with large orange plastic trash sack pumpkins filled with crumpled newspapers and white plastic trash sack ghosts suspended from the trees and front doorway. Line the walkway with ghostly luminaries (see Chapter 2).

★ Place a ghost at each place setting as a party favor (wrap a large round lollipop with a circle cut from a white plastic garbage bag, tie at the neck with a black ribbon, and draw large ghostly eyes using a black marker).

★ Decorate the room with sprayed cobwebs, orange and black balloons, crepe paper streamers, and scary jack-o-lanterns.

Amusements

★ Costume Parade—Have the children parade around the house, yard or neighborhood, showing off their costumes. Give prizes for the scariest, most creative, cutest, and so on.

★ Bobbing for Donuts or Apples—Hang sturdy donuts (glazed or buttermilk work best) from the ceiling with strings. Have the children hold their hands behind their backs as they bob for the donuts, trying to tear one loose from its string. Or, fill a large wash tub full of small Red Delicious apples and, give the children each one chance to grab an apple in their teeth using only their mouths (no hands allowed.) These are both messy activities (which is probably why the children love them), so be prepared by laying sheets of plastic over the floor beforehand.

★ Mummy Wrap (see Chapter 4).

★ Mr. Pumpkin Musical Chairs (see Chapter 24).

★ Apple Biting Contest—suspend apples from the ceiling by strings. Divide the children up into pairs, two children per apple. Ask the children to place their hands behind their backs and at a given signal begin to bite their apples. The object is to bite the apple down to its core. The difficulty, of course, is to keep the apple from swinging around as they try to take bites. The pair who has chewed their apple closest to the core at the end of three minutes is declared the winner.

✮ Younger children may enjoy a Halloween video, such as *Barney's Halloween Party, Winnie the Pooh Boo to You Too,* or *Casper Meets Wendy.*

✮ Old Dead Joe's Cave—This is a deliciously scary activity for the *older* kids. The object is to set up a darkened room ahead of time where Old Dead Joe's guts, eyes, tongue, etc. are placed in bowls. If the children are brave enough, they are blindfolded and allowed to enter the cave, one child at a time. You, as gracious host, lead the child from bowl to scary bowl, telling him to dip his hands into the bowl to feel the contents. The rest of the children sit quietly and listen intently to the screams and squeals of the child being led through the cave. Here are old dead Joe's body parts that need to be assembled ahead of time:

- Old Dead Joe's Guts—A large bowl filled with wet, slimy noodles.
- Old Dead Joe's Heart—A large peeled tomato.
- Old Dead Joe's Eyes—A small, shallow bowl of water containing two large peeled grapes.
- Old Dead Joe's Teeth—A metal pot or bowl filled with small rocks or candy corn.
- Old Dead Joe's Hair—A human hair wig sitting on a wig stand.
- Old Dead Joe's Tongue—A slimy, wet piece of raw beef liver sitting in a shallow bowl of warm water.
- Old Dead Joe's Bones—Old steak bones or any kind of bones.
- Old Dead Joe's Ears—Two halves of an artichoke (with the sharp tips cut off).
- Old Dead Joe's Nose—A raw potato carved into the shape of a nose.
- Old Dead Joe's Fingers—Cold hot dogs.
- Old Dead Joe's Blood—A crock pot full of warm tomato juice

Have a towel ready to wrap around the child's hands after he has dipped them in the "blood." As you exit the room with the child, make a big deal out of saying, "Hurry, let's wash the blood off in the sink— don't let the blood drip on the floor," and so on.

Use a small flashlight to guide your way through the dark room. Of course, the child will be blindfolded, but you'll need a little bit of light to be able to dip his hands in and out of the bowls.

✪ Tell ghost stories. Turn the lights off and have the storyteller hold a flashlight under his chin as he tells the stories. (See *Best Ghost Stories* and *The Collected Ghost Stories of Mrs. J. H. Riddell* in Resources.)

✪ Videotape all the festivities and show the tape at the end of the party. The children will especially love the part about Old Dead Joe.

Edibles

✪ Old Dead Joe's hot dogs.

✪ Old Dead Joe's chili.

✪ Old Dead Joe's potato chips.

✪ Old Dead Joe's Halloween candies.

✪ Old Dead Joe's Favorite Cupcake Spiders (see Chapter 74) or Old Dead Joe's Favorite Worm Cake. Top a chocolate sheet cake with crumbled chocolate sandwich cookies and add gummy worms crawling out of it.

✪ Old Dead Joe's foaming Pumpkin Punch (see Chapter 24). To add a floating hand, fill a rubber glove with water, tie it tightly at the wrist, and freeze solid. Remove frozen hand from glove by running under warm water and float in punch.

Tips

✪ For costume ideas, see *The Halloween Costume Book* by Katharine Thornton, and *The Halloween Book* by Jack Macguire. (See Resources.)

✪ For more Halloween games and activities, see *Halloween Fun* by Eleanor Levie. (See Resources.)

Chapter

49

Hanukkah Party

Hanukkah, also known as the Festival of Lights, is a Jewish holiday that takes place for eight days during December. Although adults are also present during this party, it is planned especially for children.

Invitations

☆ Handcrafted invitations are very special; make them in the shape of a dreidel (a top with four sides).

Decorations

☆ In addition to the display of the menorah, Jewish homes

are decorated with Hanukkah motifs, including the six-pointed Star of David.

☆ Use blue and white, the traditional Jewish colors, for crepe paper streamers, the tablecloth, napkins, paper plates, and cups.

☆ Have the children make paper chains from blue and white construction paper: Cut the paper into 1" x 8" lengths. Loop them together with glue or a stapler. String the paper chains over doorways, windows, and the light fixture over the serving table.

Activities

☆ Children and adults exchange gifts. Parents and grandparents often distribute Hanukkah gelt (money), either as real coins or as foil-wrapped chocolate coins (usually given to the younger children). Parents give gifts to their children each night of Hanukkah, usually saving the best gifts until the last night.

☆ Hanukkah games are played, including a traditional game played with the dreidel.

☆ Hanukkah songs are sung.

☆ Older family members tell stories and present riddles to the children.

Edibles

☆ Traditional Jewish foods are served, including a special delicacy, potato latkes (pancakes).

Chapter

50

Christmas Party

Christmas party is one of the easiest to host because you can take advantage of decorations you already have on display in your yard and home.

Invitations

* Attach Christmas tree ornaments to hand-printed or computer-generated invitations. Look for sled, rocking horse, or Santa ornaments.
* Attach the invitation to the front of a Christmas coloring book and mail with a box of crayons.
* Thread a candy cane through the corner of a store-bought party invitation.

Attire

☆   Encourage the children to wear red and green clothing.

Decorations

☆   In addition to your traditional Christmas decorations, make a gumdrop tree for your table or to set in a corner of the room. Suspend gum drops from the branches of any silk ficus tree or plant. Tie each branch with ribbons.

☆   Cover your serving tables with red or green felt.

☆   Make Stuffed Animal Santas: Create a centerpiece of stuffed animals wearing Santa hats. Tie red and green helium balloons to their wrists with crinkle tie ribbons. Set the animals in a snow bank (drape rolls of cotton over mounds of crumpled newspapers and flock the cotton with artificial spray snow).

☆   Wrap party favors as Christmas gifts and set one at each place setting.

Activities

☆   Let the children pop their own popcorn in the fireplace (using campfire popcorn poppers), then string it up as Christmas tree decorations they may take home with them.

☆   Christmas stocking decorating—Provide one plain, unadorned stocking for each child, along with decorating supplies: glue, glitter, stickers, ribbons, red, green and white felt squares, stick-on alphabet letters, felt-tip markers, and so forth. Give the children thirty minutes to decorate their stockings. Give them candy canes, licorice, and small toys to fill the stockings, which may be taken home as Christmas gifts.

☆   Play Pin the Nose on Rudolph, a variation of Pin the Tail on the Donkey.

☆   Insert small, numbered pieces of paper inside helium balloons tied to the backs of the guests' chairs (red for girls' gifts, green for boys'). One at a time, have the kids burst their balloons by sitting on them, then match their numbers with the gifts lying under the Christmas tree.

Edibles

☆ Santa's Kebobs (See Do-It-Yourself Shish Kebobs in Chapter 72). Let the children skewer their own kebobs and cook them over your barbecue or fireplace.

☆ Santa's Jigglers (See Jell-O Jigglers in Chapter 72).

☆ Gingerbread man cookies.

☆ Gumdrops.

☆ Ice Cream Santas: Place an upside-down ice cream cone on a red paper plate. Use canned whipped cream to squirt on Santa's beard and to trim the bottom and tip of his hat. Use two brown M&Ms for Santa's eyes and one red M&M for his mouth.

☆ Santa's Party Punch (see Heavenly Party Punch in Chapter 74).

Tip

☆ Serve the food in children's toys (Barbie convertible, dump truck, red plastic sand buckets with shovels, and so forth).

Part

5

Special Occasion Parties for Children

*I*n addition to birthdays and holidays, there are also special occasions to be celebrated. In this section you'll find ways to celebrate the arrival of a new baby sister or brother, the end of the team's season, a special achievement, and the arrival of a new kid on the block.

When your children are grown, they will remember the love and effort you put into celebrating these special occasions, which will set a precedent as they raise their own children.

Chapter

51

Super Sibling Selebration

This is a party in honor of the older sibling whose home has been invaded by a new baby brother or sister. As we all know, a new baby demands a lot of time and attention, so it's understandable that the older brother or sister may be feeling a little left out.

The format of the party is a cross between a birthday party and a shower, with the big bro or sis the center of attention.

It can be anything from a destination party (see Chapter 10) to a barbecue picnic in the park—whatever the honored guest prefers. It's a good idea to have the party somewhere other than at home, however, because nothing would kill the fun more than having to keep quiet because the new baby is sleeping!

Invitations

A Super Sibling party is a brand new idea, so you won't find ready-made invitations on the market. You can improvise, however, by hand-printing or computer generating an invitation. Here is suggested wording:

You're Invited to a Super Sibling Selebration
in honor of Jason Wilson, Brand New Big Brother
Saturday, June 10, at 1 p.m.
DePue Park [Bring your basketball, baseball, and baseball glove.]
RSVP 555-1129

Decorations

★ Decorate the party table with balloons and colorful paper cloth, napkins, plates and cups.

Amusements

★ If it's a destination party, at a bowling alley, for example, you won't need to plan anything special, other than the opening of gifts.

★ Because the idea of this party is to build the self-esteem of the older sibling, gifts are a very important element. They can be regular gifts, such as a toy or a new computer game, or humorous gifts, such as:
  - Earplugs (so he won't be kept awake with little sister's crying).
  - T-shirt (have one customized with "I'm the Awesome Big Brother" or other appropriate wording).
  - His own personal baby bottle (an oversized version can be purchased from a veterinary supply store), filled with his favorite candy.

Edibles

★ This party is in honor of the Super Sibling, so he or she should be asked what type of food should be served. If it is an outdoor party, however, you can suggest barbecued hot dogs and hamburgers, along with plenty of chips, potato salad, baked beans, and so forth.

★ An elaborate cake is in order with appropriate words written in frosting, such as "Congratulations to the World's Best Brother/Sister."

Tips

★ Make this party as big a deal as you can by inviting a lot of your child's peers.

★ This type of party is a new concept, so you may need to drop the hint to the invitees' parents that gifts would be appreciated.

Chapter

52

End-of-Season Team Party (for children)

Winning season or not, there is always a bit of a let-down when the season is finally over. So why not perk things up with an end of season party?

Invitations

☆ Cut appropriate shapes from heavy paper, representing the sport, such as a football, soccer ball, baseball, etc. Use a black felt tip marker to handprint the invitation on the back of the ball, then mail.

Attire

☆ Encourage team members to wear their uniform shirts.

152

Decorations

* ☆ Decorate with pom-poms, megaphones, and sports paraphernalia, such as soccer balls, football helmets, or field hockey sticks.
* ☆ Display game photos on a bulletin board.
* ☆ If you have a scanner hooked up to your computer, enlarge players' photos into poster-sized pictures that can be displayed around the room.

Amusements

* ☆ Take instant photos of the team members as they arrive. Display them on small easels as part of the table decorations.
* ☆ Videotape the party and play the tape toward the end, along with tapes showing outstanding plays from a few of the team's games.
* ☆ If weather permits, provide a few outdoor activities (see Chapter 3). If you have a swimming pool and it's warm outside, you won't need anything else!

Edibles

* ☆ Serve plenty of snacks—chips and salsa, popcorn, pretzels, etc.
* ☆ Serve pizza, hamburgers, hot dogs, or spaghetti, along with a green salad, French bread, and plenty of soda.
* ☆ Make or buy a cake decorated with a baseball and bat, soccer ball, football, pennant, or other appropriate symbol. It should say something like "Congratulations on a Winning Season," or "Way to Go, Cougars!"

Tip

* ☆ Be sure to involve your child in the party planning—ask what types of food and entertainment he or she would enjoy most.

Chapter

53

Achievement Celebrations for Children

Children need plenty of praise, especially when they have achieved something special, and there's no better way to pump them up than to celebrate with a party. The party doesn't need to be complicated and time-consuming to plan. In fact, it can be as simple as an afternoon at a water park with his friends, or an at-home party with his favorite eats and a congratulatory cake.

Make a big deal out of anything and everything you can—only you know what means a lot to your child in the way of individual achievement. Here are some ideas:

☆   Made the team.
☆   Voted class president.
☆   Excellent report card.
☆   Got his braces off.

☆ Won a scholarship to summer camp.

☆ Won first place in a sports competition.

Invitations

☆ Send customized, computer-generated invitations heralding the child's achievement and the details of the celebration.

Decorations

☆ Rent a neon "Congratulations" sign for your front window. (Look under Signs or Neon Signs in the Yellow Pages.)

Amusements

☆ If it's a destination party, the fun will take care of itself.

☆ If it's an at-home party, include a few of your child's favorite games (or choose a few from Chapters 3 or 4).

Edibles

☆ Ask your child what he or she would like to have served at the party and go from there. Whether it's hot dogs and macaroni and cheese, pizza, or a trip to McDonald's, try to go along with the request.

☆ If it's a braces-off party, serve all those goodies she couldn't enjoy for so long, such as corn-on-the-cob or candy apples.

Chapter

54

New-Kid-on-the-Block Party

If there is a new family in your neighborhood with a child the same age as yours, what could be nicer than to have an informal party in her honor?

Or there may be a new kid in your child's class at school, or in his Sunday School class at church. In any case, a little party in his honor will be appreciated by the child and her parents, but, most importantly, it will set an example for your child of the importance of extending friendship to newcomers.

Invitations

☆ Computer-generate invitations, or simply invite the children over the telephone.

156

Decorations

- ✯ A colorful banner can be hung over the front door saying something like, "Welcome to the Neighborhood, Michelle."
- ✯ Add a few helium-filled balloons and colorful paper plates, cups, and tablecloth.
- ✯ A decorated cake should be the focal point.

Amusements

- ✯ Ask your child what she thinks would be fun to do. You might want to include a few games from Chapters 3 or 4. The important thing is for the children to get a chance to know their new friend, and for the new kid to feel liked and accepted.

Edibles

- ✯ See Chapter 72 for creative mini-meals or order pizza. You might want to make your child's favorite meal.
- ✯ A cake that welcomes the-new-kid-on-the-block is a must—seeing her name spelled out in frosting will pump her up and make her feel good about the move and her new friends.

Special Occasion Parties for Teens

There are many special times in a teen's life—graduation day, the senior prom, the day his team wins the district finals in basketball, the day he wins the scholarship to Stanford, or the day he leaves home to join the Marines. Teen years are emotional years, and kids need to know that others care and feel their hurts and joys. So what better way to show that you care than to celebrate the special times in your teen's life? I hope the ideas in this section help you plan memorable parties for your teenage children.

Chapter
55

Post-Prom Party

Once teens have found dates to the prom, purchased gowns or rented tuxedos, and secured transportation, the issue of utmost importance becomes what to do *after* the prom. Many teens of driving age choose to caravan to hotels or vacation homes at area beaches and spend the weekend enjoying the surf and sand. Others keep it simple with a late-night snack at a local diner. Some teens, however, long to make it last by attending a party after the prom.

Whether the post-prom party is formal or informal, the kids will appreciate having something planned where they can be together, reminisce over the evening's activities, and enjoy special food.

Invitations

★ Send formal or informal invitations, depending on the type of party.

Decorations

★ Line the driveway and the entryway to your home with luminaries (see Chapter 2).

★ For a formal affair, set the table with long-stemmed toasting glasses or mugs custom-engraved with an appropriate logo, such as "Evening in the Park—Harding High Senior Prom." Give the glasses or mugs to the guests to take home as mementos of their prom night. (These are available from Anderson's Prom and Party Catalog—see Resources.)

★ Make or order an elegant floral arrangement as a centerpiece for the serving table. Turn the lights down low and illuminate the room with candles.

★ Sprinkle the table with metallic confetti in the letters P, R, O, and M, or in the shape of a dancing couple (also available from Anderson's Prom and Party Catalog).

★ For an informal affair, add balloon bouquets and colorful streamers.

Amusement

★ Take an instant photo of each couple as they arrive. Send the photo home in a frame you have constructed beforehand from poster board.

★ Show videotape of the prom (arrange to have it taped ahead of time).

Edibles

★ Depending on how late the party is, serve a midnight or breakfast buffet. Stay away from any foods that are drippy or messy.

Tip

★ Don't serve alcoholic beverages.

High School Graduation Party

A high school graduation party theme can be based on the school colors, an interest, hobby or goal of the graduate, or you can use one of the party themes included in Part 7, such as an Hawaiian Luau or a Karaoke Party.

Invitations

☆ Send diploma invitations—rolled-up parchment scrolls tied with narrow ribbon with the invitation printed inside.

☆ Make color copies of a photo of the school mascot or the honored guest as an elementary student. Write the invitation on the back.

Attire

☆ Casual attire.

162

Decorations

* If you're planning on hosting the party with other parents and you expect a big crowd, this might be one of those times you want to splurge and rent a tent, unless you live someplace where you can be pretty sure it won't rain in June.

* Decorate with oversized rolled-up diplomas and mortarboards, complete with dangling tassels.

* Decorate the serving table with high school memorabilia—prom photos, textbooks, pom-poms, pennants, yearbooks, and so on.

* Enlarge the graduate's yearbook photo to display on an easel.

* Splash the school colors around the room with crepe paper or Mylar polyester film streamers and helium balloons.

Amusements

* Ask the school mascot to make a special guest appearance.

* Ask the graduates present to tell what they will remember most about their high school years and their friendship with the guest of honor.

* Watch videotapes of the senior proms, school sports events, and the graduation ceremony itself.

* Play a roving reporter—with video recorder in hand, go up to guests and ask how they would complete the following phrase about the graduate(s) standing next to them: "most likely to...."

* Show the videotape near the end of the party.

Edibles

* See Chapters 71, 72, 73, and 74 for menu and recipe ideas, or serve traditional teen favorites, such as make-your-own tacos, spaghetti, pizza, barbecued hamburgers with all the trimmings, or giant deli sandwiches.

* Have some fun by converting your kitchen counter into a school cafeteria, serving "mystery casserole" and other lunchroom staples, or serve the refreshments in school lunch boxes or brown lunch bags.

Tips

* It's important to involve your graduate in the party plans.

* Don't serve alcohol at a high school graduation party.

Chapter
57

End-of-Season Team Party (for teens)

Whether it was a winning season or not, there's always a bit of a let down when the season is finally over. So, why not perk things up by getting the team together for a little bonding, reflection, and lots of fun!

Invitations

✰ Cut appropriate shapes from heavy paper, such as a football, soccer ball, baseball, etc. Use a black marker to print the invitation on the back of the ball, then mail.

Attire

✰ Encourage team members to wear their uniform shirts (without pads in the case of football).

164

Decorations

☆ Decorate with cheerleading pom-poms, megaphones, and sports paraphernalia, such as soccer balls, football helmets, or field hockey sticks.

☆ Place a team-colored mum plant in the center of the serving table, embellished with a pennant with the team's name (made from a poster board triangle stapled to a dowel).

☆ Display season photos on a bulletin board.

☆ If you have a scanner hooked up to your computer, enlarge players' photos into poster-sized pictures that can be displayed around the room.

Amusements

☆ Take instant photos of the team members as they arrive. Display them on small easels as part of the table decorations.

☆ Videotape the party and play the tape toward the end, along with tapes showing outstanding plays from a few of the season's games.

☆ If weather permits, provide a few outdoor activities: volleyball, badminton, horseshoes, and a basketball shooting competition. If you have a swimming pool, you won't need anything else!

☆ An End-of-Season Party definitely calls for toasts (use ginger ale or other soda) to the coach, the team, and certain players. The toasts can be serious or humorous, as long as they give tribute.

☆ You don't need to worry too much about amusing the guests—they will entertain themselves as they enjoy the relaxed team camaraderie and relive their season.

Edibles

☆ Serve plenty of snacks—chips and salsa, popcorn, pretzels, etc.

☆ Serve pizza, hamburgers, hot dogs, or spaghetti, along with a green salad and plenty of soda.

☆ Make or buy a cake decorated with a saying, such as "Congratulations on a Winning Season" or "Way to Go, Cougars," along with a baseball and bat, soccer ball, football, or other appropriate sports-related items.

Tip

☆ Be sure to involve your teen in the party planning—ask what types of food and entertainment he or she would enjoy most.

Chapter
58

Achievement Celebrations for Teens

A teenager deserves to be congratulated and pumped up a little when he or she has achieved something great, so why not throw a party to celebrate?

Make a big deal out of anything and everything you can, including:

- ☆ Winning a college scholarship.
- ☆ Winning an award for excellence in academics, sports, a school debate contest, community service, and so forth.
- ☆ Being inducted into the National Honor Society.
- ☆ Receiving his or her first driver's license.
- ☆ Buying his or her first car.

☆ Being voted class president, cheerleader, most likely to succeed, most valuable player, prom queen or king, and so on.

☆ Getting braces removed.

Invitations

☆ Send customized, computer-generated invitations heralding your teen's achievement and the details of the celebration.

Decorations

☆ Rent a neon "Congratulations" sign for your front window. (To find a rental outlet, look under Signs or Neon Signs in the Yellow Pages.)

Amusements

☆ Use one of the destination party ideas in Chapter 41 or one of the Just-for-the-Fun-of-It themes from Part 7.

Edibles

☆ This is a party to pull out all the stops and serve anything your teen suggests, even if it's barbecued steaks on the grill. Cater to his or her every whim, which will prove that you're really impressed with the achievement and want to honor him or her.

☆ If it's a braces-off party, you might suggest serving all those goodies she couldn't enjoy for so long, such as corn-on-the-cob or candy apples.

Tip

☆ Ask your teen what kind of party he or she would prefer.

Chapter
59

Farewell Party

The reason for hosting a farewell party is usually bittersweet—the person is moving away, going off to college, or perhaps leaving on a short- or long-term military or missionary assignment.

In any case, the purpose of this party is to send the person off with your love and best wishes for happiness and success. So make this party as festive as possible.

Plan a party theme around the honoree's destination, or adopt one of the ideas from Part 7.

Invitations

☆ Attach a printed invitation to a travel brochure for the destination, or

☆ Print the invitations on baggage tags, which are available at luggage stores or at your local airport.

168

Attire

☆ Casual. If you'd like, you can ask the guests to dress in outfits appropriate to your honored guest's destination, such as swimsuits, cover-ups, and beach shoes for Miami, or raincoats and umbrellas for Seattle.

Decorations

☆ Contact the Chamber of Commerce or Visitors' Bureau at your honored guest's destination city and ask for brochures, maps, and information about the city. Use these as decorations. Of course, your guest will appreciate taking them with him when he leaves. You can also pull up the city's Web site for photos and information.

☆ Use novelty decorations that reflect the destination, such as cowboy boots for Texas or "free speech" posters for Berkeley, and so forth.

Amusements

☆ Encourage the guests to offer toasts, tributes, or reminiscences.

☆ Videotape these poignant or humorous farewell speeches, play them back as part of the evening's entertainment, and then give the tape to the guest of honor as a remembrance of the party.

☆ Research the destination city and state to create a trivia game. For example, what is Tennessee's state flower? State bird? Population of Memphis? Names of adjoining states?

☆ Gifts are appropriate. Choose those that are geared toward the guest of honor's mode of travel or the destination itself. Wrap them in small moving boxes, complete with packing paper.

☆ Surprise the guest of honor with a special "This is Your Life" presentation:

This Is Your Life

Cast:
- Master of Ceremonies.
- The Guest of Honor.
- Mystery Guests (who help tell her story).

Set: A special chair for the guest of honor.

Props: A large scrapbook that says "This Is Your Life [child's name]" on the front cover.

This skit is based on the old television show, *This Is Your Life*, where the guest of honor is surprised by friends and family members who appear unexpectedly to help tell the story of the person's life.

The show begins:

Master of Ceremonies *(as he or she approaches the guest of honor)*: "Are you having a nice time at your party?"

[The guest of honor will undoubtedly answer "yes."]

"Well, it's wonderful to be honored this way by your friends and family, but we have an even bigger surprise for you: [Name], this is your life!"

(He shows her the front of the book and escorts her to her chair of honor. Someone rushes out to present her with a bouquet of flowers.)

Master of Ceremonies: "It all began in [city and state where the guest was born]."

"Mystery" Voice from Off Stage: "I remember it well—I almost didn't make it to the hospital in time."

(Out comes her mother, of course, who hugs her daughter and continues with any humorous or interesting facts relating to her daughter's birth.)

Other Voices from Off Stage (Examples):

- An aunt or other relative, who tells a story about something funny the guest of honor did when she was a little girl, or what she liked to eat, or how she found a kitten and brought it home with her, etc.

- Her sister, who tells what she was like as a kid and how she always got into her lipstick, borrowed her clothes, etc.

- Her best friend, who tells about the time they got lost in a snowstorm because she was too stubborn to stop and ask for directions.

- Her high school drama teacher, who tells about the time she had the lead in the senior play.

- The honored guest's grandmother, (or some other friend or relative who traveled a long distance to surprise her by being at the party) who tells how proud she was of her on the day she graduated from high school.

  (The mystery guests should appear in chronological order, corresponding with the events in the honored guest's life. For example, someone may tell about how sweet or ornery she was as a toddler, then the next person may tell about how she led her team to the state softball championship in high school, and so on.)

- The last guest is the honored guest's boyfriend (who has been hidden away in a back bedroom all this time.) Of course, his appearance is the best surprise of all, and brings her story to an end.

Edibles

☆ Use menu ideas from Part 9 or, if several people are co-hosting this party, plan a progressive breakfast, lunch, or dinner that includes all of the co-hosts' homes.

Part

7

Just-for-the-Fun-of-It Parties for Teens

Sometimes it's fun to plan a party just because! I don't know if you're like my husband and I are when it comes to raising teenagers, but we always wanted to have the party at our house—that way we knew where the kids were and what was going on! These fun times with our kids and their friends also gave us a closeness with our children, because they knew we were the parents who cared enough to go to the trouble to plan a party just for the fun of it.

This section includes eight teen favorites. I'm sure you'll find one your teen will love, and remember—as long as you provide plenty of their favorite foods and drinks, the party can't fail!

Chapter
60

Winter Beach Party

This is a novelty party for the cold winter months, especially in the Northeast and Midwest when temperatures dip into the teens.

Invitations

☆ Attach little beach umbrellas (tiny paper parasols) to hand-printed or computer-generated invitations, encouraging the guests to wear beach attire to the party, and assuring them the temperature in the house will be "tropical."

Attire

☆ Ask the kids to wear their swimsuits, cover-ups, sunglasses, beach shoes, and hats, and ask them to bring large beach towels.

☆ Bare feet.

172

Decorations

- ☆ Palm trees cut out of poster board, embellished with green paper fronds.
- ☆ Travel posters of warm beach destinations.
- ☆ Beach towels and umbrellas.
- ☆ Patio furniture, including tables, chairs, and chaise lounges.
- ☆ Turn the thermostat up to 80 degrees or higher.

Amusements

- ☆ Play Caribbean or Hawaiian music in the background.
- ☆ For entertainment:
  - Play pool, ping pong, or darts.
  - Watch a movie or music video.
  - Rent a karaoke machine for the evening (see Chapters 6 and 65).
  - Play one of the games from Chapter 6, such as:
    - • Dictionary Game.
    - • Communication Game.
    - • Charades or Pictionary.
    - • Observation Game.

Edibles

- ☆ Have plenty of your teen's favorite snack foods on hand.
- ☆ Order pizza and make a huge tossed salad, or
- ☆ Roast hot dogs and marshmallows over the "barbecue" (use your fireplace). Add a few old fashioned picnic dishes, such as potato salad, deviled eggs, baked beans, and watermelon.
- ☆ Serve Polynesian Smoothies (see Chapter 74) or cold soda from a galvanized tub filled with ice.
- ☆ Have s'mores or make-your-own sundaes for dessert.

Hawaiian Luau

I've found the Hawaiian Luau to be a universally popular party theme, even among teenagers. I think teens like it as much as the rest of us because it gives them a chance to hang loose and dress down, which they prefer anyway.

Invitations

* ☆   Tie the corner of each invitation to a colorful Hawaiian lei or shell necklace and mail in a padded envelope. Ask the kids to wear their leis or necklaces to the party, or
* ☆   Attach each invitation to the corner of a Hawaiian travel brochure.

Attire

* ☆   Shorts and Hawaiian shirts.
* ☆   Grass skirts and halter tops.
* ☆   Sarongs or muumuus.

☆ Colorful leis, beads, or shell necklaces.

☆ Bare feet.

☆ Flowers in the girls' hair.

Decorations

☆ Whether your party is held outdoors, which is ideal, or indoors due to inclement weather, here are some popular decorating ideas:

1. Brochures and travel posters of Hawaii (visit your travel agent).

2. Hang fishnets from the ceiling or over doorways.

3. Create displays of sand, sea shells, and driftwood (buy a sack of ordinary sandbox sand).

4. Fill the room or patio with live or silk plants that are as tropical-looking as possible.

5. Set arrangements of large, colorful fresh or silk flowers around the room.

6. Display a mural that has a Polynesian theme, such as one of several available from Anderson's Prom and Party Catalog (see Resources).

7. Decorate the patio or garden with outdoor tiki torches. (These are available in the garden department of Home Depot; they can also be rented.)

8. Large palm fronds or grass mats as place mats.

9. Large fish bowls with live goldfish as centerpieces.

10. If you have a swimming pool, float a rubber raft filled with colorful silk or fresh flowers and lighted votive candles.

11. If you can borrow or rent them, add a lava fountain, tiki statues and Hawaiian masks.

12. Wrap galvanized buckets of iced drinks with grass skirts.

Amusements

☆ Play Hawaiian background music throughout the party.

☆ If you didn't send Hawaiian leis with your

invitations, greet your guests at the door with a lei and a kiss on each cheek.

☆ If the party takes place around a pool, include swimming as an activity.

☆ Have a hula contest: Purchase inexpensive hula skirts from your favorite import store, or make them with strips of green crepe paper or plastic garbage bags. Tie skirts around a few of the guys, play recorded Hawaiian music, and see how well they can hula. (Keep your camera or video camera ready!)

☆ Give hula lessons, whether amateur or professional.

☆ Give each teen a length of flowered Hawaiian fabric, plus scissors and safety pins. Set a timer and see who can come up with the cleverest Hawaiian garment in five minutes. (They can use the fabric to make a scarf, headband, belt, hat, halter top, short sarong skirt, or anything else they can think of.)

☆ Ask a talented male lip-syncer to practice ahead of time singing to Don Ho's recordings of "Tiny Bubbles" and "Pearly Shells."

☆ Have someone sing "Lovely Hula Hands" as he plays a ukulele and the girls dance the hula.

☆ Have a hula hoop contest.

Edibles

Here's everything you need for an authentic Hawaiian luau:

☆ Roast pork.

☆ Grilled fish.

☆ Fresh pineapple slices soaked in teriyaki sauce and lightly grilled.

☆ Fresh strawberries.

☆ Melons.

☆ Papayas.

☆ Roasted bananas (peel, dip in melted butter and sprinkle with sugar; wrap in aluminum foil and roast for 20 minutes).

☆ Sweet Hawaiian bread.

☆ Bowls of sweet, fresh coconut.

☆ Boiled sweet potatoes.

☆ Fresh green salad with tomatoes, onions, raw zucchini squash, cucumbers and plenty of ripe avocados.

☆ Hawaiian fruit salad:
  - 1 cup sour cream.
  - 1 cup shredded coconut.
  - 1 cup pineapple tidbits, drained.
  - 1-1/2 cups Mandarin oranges, drained.
  - 1-1/2 cups miniature marshmallows.
  - Freshly ground nutmeg.

  Combine all ingredients except the nutmeg and let chill in refrigerator overnight. Sprinkle with nutmeg just before serving.

☆ Bowls of Macadamia nuts.

☆ Of course, a bowl of poi.

☆ Hawaiian Volcano Punch: Fill a punch bowl with fruit punch and scoops of raspberry sherbet. Pour cold raspberry soda or ginger ale over the sherbet.

☆ Polynesian Smoothies (see Chapter 74).

Tips

☆ Traditional luau food should be served from one long buffet table.

☆ This theme works best after dark, when you can light the yard with tiki torches.

Chapter

62

Tailgate Party

You don't usually think about having a tailgate party until you drive into the parking lot beside the stadium and notice those who came early and are having a great time eating barbecued chicken, enjoying cold drinks, and watching the pre-game show on their portable TVs. So, if your teenager and his or her friends have tickets to a concert or ballgame, why not use that as your excuse to throw the best tailgate party your kids have ever seen! You'll be the most popular parents in town!

Invitations

☆ Use postcards with a picture of a car as your invitations, or take a photo of your car with the tailgate down (if you have a station wagon, hatchback, SUV or pickup truck) or the trunk open, with a blanket or checkered tablecloth spread out and topped with picnic basket and ice chest. Write the invitation on the back of the postcard or photo and mail.

178

Decorations

★ A tailgate party needs no ambiance—the novelty of the event is enough. However, it has become trendy to dress up a tailgate party (in a tongue-in-cheek kind of way) with tablecloths, balloons, a wildflower bouquet, and any other decorations you would like to include, such as trailing ivy to frame the tailgate or trunk.

★ You can coordinate your tailgate party with sturdy plastic plates, cups, serving bowls, and tablecloth of the same color.

Amusements

★ Bring a boom box with tapes or CDs of the concert performer or a portable TV to watch the pre-game coverage of a sports event.

Edibles

★ Set up your portable barbecue and cook steaks, hamburgers, hot dogs, roasted potatoes or corn-on-the-cob.

★ Bring an ice chest filled with fried chicken, macaroni salad, cold veggies and dips, cheeses, canned juices, and soda.

★ Serve potato chips, cookies, and hot chocolate.

★ Don't forget the condiments: catsup, mustard, steak sauce, relish, pickles, olives, butter, salt, and pepper.

★ Bring utensils: barbecue tools, a bottle opener, a sharp carving knife, steak knives (if applicable), serving forks and spoons, and plenty of cloth napkins or paper towels.

★ A few TV trays will come in handy.

Tips

★ If there will be several carloads of teens at your party, have them park their cars or trucks in a semicircle for the ultimate in tailgate bonding.

★ Bring plenty of blankets, garbage bags, and folding lawn chairs.

Video Scavenger Hunt

This is one of the most popular party themes going these days, especially among the teen set.

The idea is to divide the kids into groups of four to six each (enough to fill one car). The groups compete against each other to see which one can return first having videotaped every required scene or stunt on the scavenger hunt list.

You'll need to provide one video camera and tape per group, along with the list of required scenes and stunts. Of course, there will need to be one licensed driver per car, so this idea won't work for younger teens unless there are several adults to help out.

Invitations

☆   Have copies made of an enlarged photo of a humorous stunt or scene; write the invitation on the back of each and mail in a photo mailer.

Attire

★ Casual and comfortable enough to perform the stunts required.

Decorations

★ Set up folding chairs theater-style in front of your TV.

★ Tie a couple of balloon bouquets to the chairs.

★ Decorate your ice cream sundae bar with balloons, colorful plastic bowls, and napkins.

Amusements

You can come up with any scenes or stunts you would like, but to give you an idea of what seems to work, here are stunts that have been required at some recent parties:

★ One of the kids in the group standing in front of (or sitting on) a statue.

★ Several members of the group joining a street entertainer in his or her act.

★ A stranger singing the national anthem.

★ All the team members eating ice cream cones.

★ One team member milking a cow.

★ One or more members of a group standing under a public clock at a certain time.

★ A member of the group singing "I Wish I Were an Oscar Meyer Weiner" while standing in the hot dog section of a local grocery store.

★ A member of the group standing on a surfboard.

★ All team members inside an elevator.

★ Any stranger from any state you would like other than your own.

★ Members of the group standing in front of a lighted outdoor Christmas tree, or waving an American flag, or offering a box of Valentine's candy, or carrying an Easter basket while pretending to search for Easter eggs, depending on the season.

★ A team member standing next to a picture of Colonel Sanders.

★ Going to the home of a friend, abducting the person, and bringing him or her back to the party with you.

★ Team members standing or sitting on a fire engine.

★ Carrying a stranger's groceries to her car.

★ A stranger trying to spell potato (or any other word you would like).

★ Opening a store door for a stranger while asking for a tip.

☆ All team members standing knee-deep in a lake, pond, or swimming pool.

☆ Asking a stranger to recite the names of all the continents.

☆ One or more members of the group singing at a karaoke bar.

☆ Reading a book or reciting a poem to a stranger.

☆ A stranger demonstrating the Macarena.

☆ Finding a stranger named Bob.

☆ Finding a stranger who knows your state flower.

☆ Finding a stranger who can imitate John Wayne.

☆ A policeman drawing a chalk line on the ground around one of the members of your group.

☆ Going up to a stranger at a service station, filling his car with gas, washing his windows, and checking his oil.

☆ Standing beside a tombstone.

☆ Standing by the greeter at a Wal Mart and greeting the customers.

☆ Spelling a certain word with your bodies while standing in front of a library.

☆ Washing dishes at a restaurant.

☆ Singing an Elvis song while standing under a neon sign.

☆ Holding a chicken.

These are examples of the types of stunts you'll need to add to your list, but I'm sure you can come up with dozens more of your own. The list should contain no more than 15 or 20 stunts total because each carload will be given only an hour and a half to videotape as many as they can. The guests are given an exact time they must return to the party venue. If not back on time, the group is disqualified.

Once every group has returned, the videotapes are played back, with each stunt scored by all the guests present on a point system from 1 to 3:

1. The stunt was videotaped, whether it was done well or not.

2. The stunt showed some creativity.

3. The stunt was exceptionally creative.

Five bonus points are given to a group if they came up with an original stunt of their own. The team with the most total points wins.

Edibles

☆ Serve snacks, appetizers, and cold or hot beverages before the hunt, while the guests are waiting for everyone to arrive and the game rules are being explained.

☆ Serve make-your-own sundaes while the kids are watching the videos after the hunt (see Chapter 73).

Chapter
64

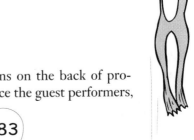

No-Talent Talent Show

Remember Amateur Night at summer camp, when kids performed skits, sang, played instruments, told jokes, recited a silly poem, or demonstrated some amazing one-of-a-kind feat? Well, that's the idea behind this theme.

This talent show needs to be as light and silly as it can be—in fact, the winners are the acts that show the least talent! There are three judges, who "gong" the contestants at the ends of their acts. One gong is good, two gongs are better, but three gongs go to the acts that demonstrate the least talent of all.

Invitations

☆ Print the invitations on the back of programs that announce the guest performers, awards they have won, how they are known all around the world for their talents, and so forth.

Attire

- ☆ Performing guests should wear their stage costumes.
- ☆ A master of ceremonies should wear a tux and top hat as he introduces each act as seriously as possible.

Decorations

- ☆ Purchase a large white poster board and use a black marker to create a program of the evening's entertainment. Set this on an easel in the rear of the room for the kids to see as they arrive.

- ☆ Set up chairs in a theater-in-the-round style, with a raised stage if possible. Darken the room and have ushers use flashlights to lead guests to their seats.

Amusements

Line up the acts in advance, such as:

- ☆ Karaoke singing (provide a toy microphone sprayed silver).
- ☆ Performing in a kazoo or hillbilly band.
- ☆ Telling jokes.
- ☆ Reciting silly poems or limericks.
- ☆ Performing magic.
- ☆ Singing.
- ☆ Dancing.
- ☆ Playing an instrument.
- ☆ Lip-syncing to a humorous song.
- ☆ A whistling choir. (Ask the whistlers in the crowd to enter their choir in the contest.)
- ☆ A comb-and-tissue-paper orchestra.
- ☆ A novelty act.

☆ Performing an improvised skit. (Provide large grocery sacks filled with such props as a cowboy hat, ukulele, mustache, can of beans, swim trunks, snorkel, Frisbee, toy gun, hairbrush, and so on. Each group must make up a skit on the spot using whatever props are contained in the sack they have selected.) Remember: There are no rules for this party. Anything goes! Survey your potential guest list and see what you can come up with.

☆ Present awards for worst musical group, least creative, etc., according to the number of gongs each contestant receives.

☆ Videotape the acts. Show the tape near the end of the party.

Edibles

☆ Serve drinks and bags of popcorn during the performances, followed later in the evening with a make-your-own sundae bar (see Chapter 73).

Tip

☆ This type of party needs a big crowd to be successful—at least 30 guests.

Chapter

65

Karaoke Party

Akaroke party is a popular party for teens. Some like to sing to the karaoke machine; others enjoy listening or acting as "celebrity judges."

If you aren' t familiar with the concept, a karaoke machine provides the words and professional musical accompaniment for popular songs, which helps (almost) anyone sound good when they sing.

Invitations

☆ Attach the invitation to a child's toy microphone and mail in a padded envelope.

Attire

★ Ask the guests to dress as "stars," as in *Star Search*.

Decorations

★ Lighted marquee in the front entry of your home, announcing auditions.

★ Enlarged sheets of sheet music.

★ CDs and glittery stars suspended from the ceiling with thin fishing line.

★ Real or toy drum sets and other instruments displayed around the room.

★ Create a stage setting by placing folding chairs in rows in front of a spotlighted microphone.

Amusements

★ Rent a karaoke machine (look under Disc Jockeys or Party Rentals in the Yellow Pages).

★ Provide a toy microphone spray-painted silver.

★ Interview the "celebrities" before they sing.

★ Encourage as many teens as possible to give it a try. Usually one or two will have sung to a karaoke machine before, and with just a little encouragement, they'll be glad to demonstrate how the concept works. The next thing you know, they're really enjoying themselves, which will encourage the others to take a chance.

★ Have a panel of judges who may "gong" a contestant, or may award prizes for the most professional, most creative, most bizarre, funniest, and so on.

★ Videotape the evening's performances; show the tape at the end of the party.

Edibles

★ During the performances, you can serve oversized drinks and bags of popcorn, followed later in the evening by a light supper or dessert buffet (see Chapter 73).

Chapter
66

Couch Potato Party

This is a party that takes place in front of the TV, so you'll need to drag in your comfortable lawn chaises and any other cushy chairs or recliners you can move in from other rooms. The idea is to make a party out of watching something special on TV, whether it's a sports event, awards show, beauty pageant, or rented movie or concert.

Invitations

☆ Mail or hand-deliver invitations attached to potatoes wrapped with ribbons. (Gift-wrap the potatoes before mailing or delivering.)

Attire

☆ The kids will be grubbing around all night, so ask them to dress way, way down.

Decorations

☆ Decorate according to what you'll be watching. If it's a music awards show, hang posters of favorite recording artists or a list of the nominees. For Emmy or Oscar night, display blown-up magazine photos of the nominees. When it comes to the Super Bowl, NBA finals, World Series, or other sports event, display banners, flags, pennants, and pom-poms in the team's colors.

Amusements

☆ Furnish ballots to the guests as they arrive so they can vote on the evening's nominees, sports teams, MVP, and so on. Award prizes to winning ballots.

Edibles

☆ Before everyone settles in for the show, serve huge baked potatoes (of course!) with all the toppings: chili, spaghetti sauce, grated cheese, sour cream, chopped onions, sliced olives, bacon bits, and so on, along with hot garlic bread and a Watermelon Boat (see Chapter 72).

☆ For dessert, serve Puddin' Parfaits (see Chapter 73).

☆ During the show, provide cold drinks and lots of snacks, such as pop-corn, chips and dips, pretzels, mixed nuts, and trail mix (see Chapter 71).

Tip

☆ Create a "couch potato paradise" by covering chaises, chairs, and reclin-ers with soft, comfortable quilts and tossing around plenty of throw pillows.

Part 8

School, Church, and Youth Group Parties

Many of you out there are clamoring for some good ideas for larger parties. This section includes three all-time favorites for large school, church, or youth groups: a carnival, indoor olympics, and a field day. I have also included a chapter called "Mix 'n Match," which gives you an opportunity to put a large group party together by combining other themes, games, and menus found in this book.

You'll find that many themes will also work for a large group, such as the Super Scavenger Hunt or the West 'n Wild Water Party. Likewise, games and activities included in many of the theme parties will work for large groups as well. Therefore, I have put them together for you in the "Mix 'n Match" chapter.

Have fun planning the party for your group, and remember: A large group party requires some help—don't try to do everything by yourself!

191

Chapter

67

Carnivals

A carnival is a popular party theme for a large group of children from a church, school, or club. It can also be called "A Day on the Board-walk" or "An Afternoon at the Penny Arcade." The idea is to keep all the children busy all the time by providing booths with competitive games, activities, and food. The carnival can become a fundraiser by selling tickets to the event or for individual games or activities, or it can be a free event by providing less complicated and less expensive activities.

A carnival, like any event for a large number of children, requires a committee of volunteers to plan the activities and staff the booths. Don't try to plan the entire thing by yourself.

Decorations

☆ Attach colorful balloons and crepe paper streamers to entrances and booths.

192

Activities

There are companies who sell pre-planned, pre-packaged "instant carnivals," such as U. S. Toy Company (see Resources). For example, they have packages of prizes and three to 12 booths for groups of up to 1,000 people, for $50 to $200. They also sell individual arcade-type games, such as a shooting gallery that includes the target and 12 cork guns for about $35. Here are ideas for carnival booths:

☆ Ticket booth: a cardboard refrigerator box with a window cut out of the front for selling or giving out free tickets.

☆ Darts.

☆ Penny toss: Give each contestant 10 pennies; set up a table full of odd-sized containers, such as empty soup cans, jars, milk cartons, etc., and award prizes based on the number of pennies that land in the containers.

☆ Frisbee toss through a suspended hula hoop.

☆ Football passing contest through a suspended tire.

☆ Ring toss.

☆ Horseshoes.

☆ Bowling.

☆ Milk bottle toss.

☆ Beanbag toss.

☆ Fish pond.

☆ Basketball free-throw contest.

☆ Squirt the candle.

☆ Make-up or face-painting booths.

☆ Tattoo booth with stick-on, removable body tattoos for children.

☆ Balloon dart game.

☆ Pie-throwing booth.

☆ Water dunking.

☆ Putting contests.

☆ Water-balloon toss.

☆ Caricaturist booth.

- ☆ Costume photo booth.
- ☆ Balloon art booth.
- ☆ Horse or pony rides.
- ☆ Tractor and wagon rides.
- ☆ Petting zoo.
- ☆ A "Jump Delight."
- ☆ Airplane toss: Pre-made paper airplanes are thrown through a suspended hula hoop.
- ☆ Food booths: Cotton candy, popcorn, snow cones, hot dogs, drinks, and so on.

To save money, you can create your own booths from cardboard appliance boxes, moving boxes, and moving wardrobe boxes, or you can have some events take place inside a fenced area or out in the open. You can also put your own arcade games together by providing a basketball hoop on a portable stand, creating your own horseshoe pit, having a beanbag toss, and so forth.

You'll also need to provide prizes or ribbons. These can be purchased inexpensively in bulk from such catalogs as U. S. Toy Company, Sally Distributors, or Oriental Trading Company (see Resources).

Edibles

- ☆ Food and drinks are available at the food booths.

Tip

- ☆ Play calliope or march music in the background during the entire carnival.

Chapter
68

Indoor Olympics

An indoor olympics needs a lot of room. A gym or empty school cafeteria will work well, as will any other recreational room, such as an empty meeting hall in a church.

This event is competitive, with prizes or ribbons (see Resources for the U.S. Toy catalog). You'll need to organize as many competitive events as necessary to fill your time span, allowing time for serving a meal and/or dessert.

Decorations

* ☆ Attach colorful balloons and crepe paper streamers to doorways.

Activities

* ☆ Dart game.
* ☆ Ring toss.
* ☆ Bowling (with plastic pins).
* ☆ Milk bottle toss.
* ☆ Beanbag toss.
* ☆ Basketball toss.
* ☆ Balloon dart game.
* ☆ Spoon race (see Chapter 4).
* ☆ Tennis ball race (see Chapter 4).
* ☆ Straw and ball race (see Chapter 4).
* ☆ Lemon race (see Chapter 4).
* ☆ Kiddy limbo (see Chapter 4).

Edibles

* ☆ Iced soda, juices, or sports drinks in coolers or galvanized tubs.
* ☆ See Part 9 for snack, meal, or dessert ideas.

Chapter

69

Field Day

A field day needs outdoor space, preferably a school yard or public park that has basketball courts, horseshoe pits, and so forth.

Decorations

☆ Tie colorful balloons and crepe paper streamers to trees, gates, and fences.

Activities

Here are competitive events you can include in your field day fun:

☆ Basketball throw contest.

- ★ Horseshoe throwing contest.
- ★ Relay races (while balancing a book on your head; while squeezing a tennis ball tightly between your knees; while placing one foot directly in front of the other).
- ★ Softball throw.
- ★ Three-legged races.
- ★ 50-yard dash.
- ★ Burlap sack races (see Chapter 3).
- ★ Obstacle course relay race (see Chapter 3).
- ★ Frisbee golf (see Chapter 6).
- ★ Tennis ball baseball (see Chapter 3).
- ★ Raw egg race (see Chapter 4).
- ★ Straw and ball race (see Chapter 4).
- ★ Lemon Race (see Chapter 4).
- ★ Standing broad jump contests.
- ★ High jump contests.
- ★ Discus throw (use metal pie pan or a Frisbee).

You'll need prizes or ribbons for the winners. The prizes don't need to be expensive; see U.S. Toy Company catalog.

Edibles

- ★ Iced soda, juices, or sports drinks in coolers or galvanized tubs.
- ★ Hot dogs, picnic food, or snacks (see Chapter 71).

Chapter
70

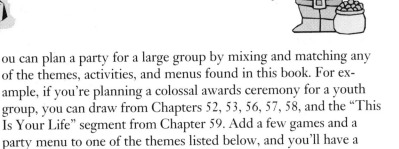

Mix 'n Match Parties

You can plan a party for a large group by mixing and matching any of the themes, activities, and menus found in this book. For example, if you're planning a colossal awards ceremony for a youth group, you can draw from Chapters 52, 53, 56, 57, 58, and the "This Is Your Life" segment from Chapter 59. Add a few games and a party menu to one of the themes listed below, and you'll have a great party.

I have assembled ideas into three categories, each divided into age groups. Choose one idea from each of these three categories:

Themes

Young Children

- ✻ Teddy Bear Party (Chapter 13).
- ✻ Dinosaur Party (Chapter 21).
- ✻ Cowboy or Cowgirl Barbecue (Chapter 23).
- ✻ October Pumpkin Party (Chapter 24).
- ✻ Wet 'n Wild Water Party (Chapter 26).
- ✻ Valentine's Day Party (Chapter 45).
- ✻ St. Patrick's Day Party (Chapter 46).
- ✻ Halloween Party (Chapter 48).
- ✻ Christmas Party (Chapter 50).
- ✻ Hanukkah Party (Chapter 49).

Older Children

- ✻ Wild West Party (Chapter 34).
- ✻ Super Scavenger Hunt (Chapter 37).
- ✻ Aloha Party (Chapter 39).
- ✻ Valentine's Day Party (Chapter 45).
- ✻ St. Patrick's Day Party (Chapter 46).
- ✻ Halloween Party (Chapter 48).
- ✻ Hanukkah Party (Chapter 49).

- ✻ Christmas Party (Chapter 50).

Teens

- ✻ Hawaiian Luau (Chapter 61).
- ✻ No-Talent Talent Show (Chapter 64).
- ✻ Karaoke Party (Chapter 65).
- ✻ Halloween Party (Chapter 48).
- ✻ Christmas Party (Chapter 50).

Activities

Young Children

- ✻ Barber Shop (Chapter 4).
- ✻ Mummy Wrap (Chapter 4).
- ✻ Shoe Basket (Chapter 4).
- ✻ Untie the Knots (Chapter 4).
- ✻ Ping Pong Ball Hunt (Chapter 4).
- ✻ Spoon Race (Chapter 4).
- ✻ Straw and Ball Race (Chapter 4).
- ✻ Lemon Race (Chapter 4).
- ✻ Kazoo Marching Band (Chapter 5).
- ✻ Fisherman's Net (Chapter 3).
- ✻ Obstacle Course Relay Race (Chapter 3).
- ✻ Musical Statues (Chapter 4).
- ✻ Kiddy Limbo (Chapter 4).
- ✻ Face Painting (Chapter 7).
- ✻ Children's Sing-Along (Chapter 5).

Older Children

- ☆ Mummy Wrap (Chapter 4).
- ☆ Shoe Basket (Chapter 4).
- ☆ Untie the Knots (Chapter 4).
- ☆ Ping Pong Ball Hunt (Chapter 4).
- ☆ Spoon Race (Chapter 4).
- ☆ Fisherman's Net (Chapter 3).
- ☆ Obstacle Course Relay Race (Chapter 3).
- ☆ Shoelace Hop (Chapter 3).
- ☆ Straw and Ball Race (Chapter 4).
- ☆ Lemon Race (Chapter 4).
- ☆ Musical Statues (Chapter 4).
- ☆ Kiddy Limbo (Chapter 4).
- ☆ Face Painting (Chapter 7).
- ☆ Tennis Ball Baseball (Chapter 3).

Teens

- ☆ Wheelbarrow Race (Chapter 3).
- ☆ Tug O' War (Chapter 3).
- ☆ Frisbee Golf (Chapter 6).
- ☆ Beach Ball Baseball (Chapter 3).
- ☆ Burlap Sack Race (Chapter 3).

Menus

Here are popular foods to serve for large groups of all ages:

- ☆ Hot dogs/hamburgers.
- ☆ Hero sandwiches (Chapter 72).
- ☆ Pizzas.
- ☆ Tacos.
- ☆ Corn dogs.
- ☆ Watermelon Boats (Chapter 72).
- ☆ Rice Krispie Squares (Chapter 73).
- ☆ Popcorn balls (Chapter 71).
- ☆ Snow cones (Chapter 73).
- ☆ Dirt Pies (Chapter 73).
- ☆ Gummy Worm Cakes (Chapter 73).
- ☆ Cupcake Spiders (Chapter 73).
- ☆ Root beer floats (Chapter 74).
- ☆ Hot cider/hot chocolate (Chapter 74).
- ☆ Non-Alcoholic Smoothies (Chapter 74).
- ☆ Heavenly Party Punch (Chapter 74).

Other popular dishes for large parties:

- ☆ Spaghetti.
- ☆ Enchiladas.
- ☆ Macaroni and cheese.
- ☆ Lasagne.

Part 9

Menus and Recipes

*T*he key to the success of any party, whether for children or adults, is to serve mouth-watering, eye-appealing food and beverages.

This section is filled with recipes for children's favorite party foods. There's everything from Peanut Butter Banana Dogs and Dirt Pies to Edible Headbands and Bug Punch. And best of all, the recipes are quick and easy to put together!

Tips
★ Eat outdoors whenever possible.
★ Don't serve nuts, hard candies, or hot dogs to small children because of the hazard of choking.
★ Have alternative treats available for any children with special dietary needs due to diabetes, lactose intolerance, or food allergies.

Chapter
71

Party Snacks

H ere are a few easy snack ideas for children's parties:

Popcorn Balls

Roll six cups of popped corn in eight ounces of melted caramel mixed with one tablespoon butter (microwave for one minute on high to melt the caramel). Shape the coated popcorn into small balls. Wrap each in plastic wrap and tie with a bow.

Snack Kabobs

Skewer chunks of cheese, pineapple, cherry tomatoes, melon balls, bananas, etc. onto wooden skewers.

Popcorn Roasted Over the Fire

Let the children pop their own popcorn over the fire using a campfire popcorn popper.

Painted Toast

Let the children paint pictures or faces on bread with food coloring, then toast.

Celery Stuffed with Peanut Butter

Wash celery stalks and pat dry; fill with peanut butter. Cut into 3" pieces and serve.

Hamburgers-in-a-Biscuit

Bake refrigerated baking powder biscuits. Cook small hamburgers. Use the biscuits as buns—add ketchup, mustard, or relish.

Bowls of Sugared Cereal

Children love to snack on sugared cereal served dry in attractive serving bowls.

Pigs-in-a-Blanket

Wrap small wieners in strips of ready-to-use crescent roll dough. Bake at 400 degrees until lightly browned on top.

Bugs-in-the-Swamp

Press raisins onto cream cheese in celery sticks.

Roasted Snake

Roll refrigerator biscuit dough into a long snake and wrap it around a metal skewer. Roast it over an open fire or barbecue until golden brown. Slide off skewer, pour softened butter and honey inside the snake and eat!

Trail Mix

Combine raisins, peanuts, M&Ms, Wheat Chex, dried apples, chopped dried apricots, coconut flakes, sunflower seeds, and pretzel sticks.

Veggies and dips

Serve bite-size pieces of broccoli, cauliflower, celery, carrots, cherry tomatoes, raw zucchini, and radishes with bowls of salad dressings.

Rice Cake Surprise

Serve rice cakes with a variety of toppings, including peanut butter, honey, jelly, yogurt, and canned puddings.

Other snacks

- ☆ Fortune Cookies
- ☆ Boxes of Animal Crackers

Chapter

72

Mini-Meals for Children's Parties

Children's parties require gimmicky names for the food. This chapter includes good ideas for mini-meals.

Poison Spider Salad

Spread each plate with large lettuce leaves. Place a large canned pear half upside down on top of the lettuce. Press hot cinnamon candies into the tops of the pear halves. Add licorice or black pipe cleaner legs.

Pineapple Boat Kebobs

Hollow out half of a fresh pineapple and fill with pineapple chunks, maraschino cherries, grapes, banana slices, cheese, and ham chunks, all skewered with cocktail picks or ruffled toothpicks.

Watermelon Boat

Cut a watermelon in half. Scoop the watermelon out in balls, using a melon baller. Place the watermelon balls back into the shell, along with mini-scoops of raspberry sherbet.

Jell-O Jigglers

Pour Jell-O into a shallow pan. When gelled, cut into squares or shapes using a knife or cookie cutters. Or pour Jell-O into small paper cups, drop one gummy bear into each one, and set in the refrigerator. When ready to serve, place the cups in lukewarm water for a few seconds and unmold them onto a serving plate.

Make-Your-Own Fruit Kabobs

Provide one wooden skewer per child, along with bowls of bite-sized fresh fruits, such as pineapple, grapes, melon balls, orange sections, strawberries, and cherries. Decorate the end of each skewer with crinkle ribbon. Let each child create his own kabob.

Hot Dogs and Beans

Let the children roast their own hot dogs over a campfire or the flames in your fireplace. Tuck them into buns, add a little mustard, and serve alongside a mound of baked beans.

Bean Boats

Split hamburger buns and place them with surface up on cookie sheets. Butter the buns and top with layers of canned pork and beans, grated cheddar cheese, and real bacon bits. Place under broiler until bubbling and browned.

Waffle Surprise

Toast two frozen waffles. Spread one with pineapple cream cheese and raspberry jam, the other with chunky peanut butter and chopped peanuts. Put the two halves together and serve.

Do-It-Yourself Shish Kabobs

Provide the children with metal barbecue skewers, plus bowls of bite-sized pineapple, brown-and-serve sausage links, French bread slices, baked ham, bananas, apples, and tomatoes. Let the children skewer their own kabobs, cover with butter-flavored cooking spray, and cook over a barbecue or campfire. (The meats have been pre-cooked so there is no fear of undercooked foods.)

Peanut Butter Banana Dogs

Fill a foot-long hot dog bun with sliced bananas, peanut butter, chopped nuts, and M&M candies.

Happy Hamburgers and Potato Chips or French Fries

Serve hamburgers with the trimmings and chips or fries. Make happy faces on the tops of the hamburger buns: use olives for eyes, squeeze mustard for eyebrows, and a chunk of celery for the nose, and finish with a slice of tomato for the mouth.

Personal Potato Toppers

Provide one baked potato per child, along with such toppings as hot chili, sour cream, crumbled bacon, cooked hamburger with taco seasoning, grated cheeses, crumbled tortilla chips, and sliced black olives. Let each child create his own potato meal.

Hero Sandwiches

Slice a whole loaf of French bread in half lengthwise. Let the children help you fill it with lunchmeats, pepperoni, sliced cheeses, sliced tomatoes, mustard, relish, pickle slices, lettuce, etc. Then, place the "lid" on the sandwich and make a big deal out of cutting it into child-sized pieces as the children watch.

Giant Pancake with Fruit Topping

Cook giant pancakes in a round cast-iron skillet. Serve in the skillet topped with fresh berries and piles of whipped cream.

Animal Sandwiches

Cut sandwiches into animal shapes using a cookie cutter.

Macaroni and Cheese

From a box or homemade, kids love this stuff!

Personalized Pizzas

Prepare individual 8" pizzas using refrigerated pizza dough, canned pizza sauce, and shredded mozzarella and cheddar cheeses. Make faces with cherry tomato noses, sliced green pepper lips, and black olive eyes. Bake according to pizza dough directions on package.

Mini-Muffin Pizzas

Give the children English muffins, along with grated cheeses, tomato sauce, sliced black olives, pepperoni pieces, etc. Let the children design their own mini-pizzas.

Make-Your-Own Taco Bar

Lay out large, heated taco shells and all the ingredients—cooked ground beef, chopped tomatoes, shredded lettuce, diced green chilies, chopped olives, shredded cheeses, salsa, and sour cream.

Chapter

73

Party Desserts

The desserts in this chapter have been kid-tested. They are all-time party favorites.

S'mores

Let the children roast large marshmallows over a fire, using sticks or straightened coat hangers. As soon as the marshmallows begin to brown, help the children squash them and half a chocolate bar between two graham crackers.

Snowballs

Roll scoops of firm vanilla ice cream in flaky coconut.

Marshmallow Fondue Dip

This is *very* messy, so you might want to take this project to the patio! Provide fondue forks, large marshmallows, and a fondue pot full of warm chocolate sauce. Let the children skewer the marshmallows, dip them into the chocolate and eat them. Variation: You can also provide fresh fruits for dipping—strawberries, orange sections, or sliced bananas.

Pudding Sandwiches

Use store-bought ready-made pudding as a filler between two graham crackers for each sandwich.

Make-Your-Own Magic Mountains

Let the kids build their own Magic Mountains. Give them graham crackers, several flavors of canned icing, marshmallow creme, plastic knives, and bowls full of dried fruits, nuts, and candy bits. Prepare the fruit and candy bits ahead of time by snipping the fruit and candy into small pieces with a pair of sharp scissors. Suggestions: Raspberry and licorice ropes, jelly beans, sprinkles, minimarshmallows, cherries, banana chips, dried apricots, raisins, macadamia nuts, peanuts, and slivered almonds.

Frozen Fruit Balls

Cut the top off a large orange. Cut out the fruit. Decorate the empty orange shells with happy faces, using black permanent markers. Fill the shells with scoops of orange sherbet and freeze until ready to serve.

Edible Headbands

Sew wrapped candies together using long strands of dental floss cut into headband lengths, with three or four inches left over for tying together. Tie a piece of curled crinkle ribbon at each juncture of candy, hiding the dental floss and decorating the headband.

Rocky Road Sandwiches

Slice chocolate cupcakes in half to make a top and bottom for each sandwich. Place a small scoop of rocky road ice cream between the halves, press together, and serve.

Make-Your-Own Sundaes

Provide bowls, several flavors of ice cream, ice cream scoops, chocolate, caramel, and strawberry sauces, maraschino cherries, crushed pineapple, sliced bananas and strawberries, nuts, and whipped cream.

Snow Ice Cream

Combine a quart of *clean* snow from your yard with one cup whole milk, a 1/2 cup sugar and 2 teaspoons vanilla. Eat immediately.

Popsicles

You can buy them or make your own by hollowing out orange halves, filling with fruit juice, and freezing.

Rice Krispie Squares

Follow the recipe on the back of the Rice Krispies box.

Frozen Bananas on a Stick

Peel bananas, cut them in half, skewer each half with a wooden stick, and freeze. Let the kids dip them in chocolate or butterscotch syrups, chunky peanut butter, honey, or soft vanilla ice cream.

Snow Cones

Fill paper cups with clean snow or crushed ice from the blender and add flavored syrup or fruit juice.

Tasty Party Necklaces

Provide long, thin strands of licorice and bowls of donut-shaped dry cereals, such as Cheerios and Trix. Let the children make their own party necklaces by threading the licorice through the cereal pieces and tying the ends together with a double knot.

Decorate-Your-Own Cupcakes

Place a plastic tablecloth over your table. Set out cupcakes, frostings, frosting tubes, sprinkles and novelty cake decorations. Give the children plastic knives and let them decorate their own cupcakes.

Ice Cream Babies

- ☆ Two gallons strawberry ice cream.
- ☆ Shredded coconut.
- ☆ Red food coloring.
- ☆ One tiny plastic baby per guest (available at party supply stores).
- ☆ White doilies.

Tint the shredded coconut pink with a few drops of red food coloring. Use a large tea cup to scoop strawberry ice cream onto a cookie sheet, forming wide, flat "skirts." Coat each skirt with the pink coconut. Insert one baby doll into the center of each skirt, cover with waxed paper, and freeze until ready to serve. Serve on white doilies.

Easter Basket Cupcakes

Bake cupcakes in pastel colored cupcake papers. Frost cupcakes with white frosting and sprinkle with white or tinted coconut flakes. Press six or eight jelly beans into the coconut flakes. Cut red licorice vines into 7" lengths. Bend these lengths into "handles" for the "baskets."

Doll Buggy Eclairs

- ✯   One eclair per guest (purchased from your favorite bakery).
- ✯   Round red and white peppermint candies.
- ✯   White pipe cleaners.
- ✯   Tiny plastic babies.
- ✯   White paper doilies.

Press the peppermint candies against each eclair, creating four "wheels." Bend a single pipe cleaner to form a handle. Cut a small slit at one end of the top of the eclair. Insert a plastic doll into the eclair at the slit, its head sticking out over the "blanket." Set each eclair on a paper doily.

Dirt Pie

- ✯   One small clay flower pot per guest.
- ✯   One large plastic drinking straw per guest.
- ✯   Rocky road ice cream.
- ✯   Oreo cookies.
- ✯   Single-stemmed fresh flowers, preferably daisies, tulips, or daffodils.

Wash flower pots well and let them dry thoroughly. Place one Oreo over the hole at the bottom of each pot. Fill each pot with rocky road ice cream to within one inch from the top. Insert a straw in the center of the ice cream and cover the rest with crushed Oreo cookies. Freeze until time to serve. Insert the stem of one fresh flower into each straw before serving.

Gummy Worm Cake

Bake any kind of cake or cupcakes. Press gummy worms down inside the cake after it has baked. Frost the cake and add more gummy worms on top.

Cupcake Spiders

Remove the paper from a chocolate cupcake. Frost the top and sides of the cupcake with thick white icing. Add eight black licorice "legs" (four on each side), chocolate sprinkles, and hot cinnamon candies for the eyes.

Do-it-Yourself Waffles

Let the children prepare their own waffles by toasting round frozen waffles in the toaster and topping them with fresh fruit, chocolate chips, gumdrops, powdered sugar, instant puddings, sundae syrups, and canned whipped topping.

Puddin' Parfaits

Mix up instant pudding according to the recipe on the box. Alternate pudding with fresh fruit in a clear pedestal glass. (For example, tapioca pudding and fresh strawberries, vanilla pudding and blueberries, chocolate pudding and sliced bananas, etc.) Top with a dollop of whipped cream or Cool Whip.

Sugar Cookies

- ☆ 1 cup melted butter.
- ☆ 1/2 cup sifted confectioners' sugar.
- ☆ 1 egg.
- ☆ 1 1/2 tsp. vanilla.
- ☆ 2 1/2 cups all-purpose flour, sifted.
- ☆ 1 tsp. baking soda.
- ☆ 1 tsp. cream of tartar.
- ☆ Canned white frosting.
- ☆ Food colorings.
- ☆ 1/4" ribbon.

Mix the first four ingredients together thoroughly. Sift the flour, baking soda, and cream of tartar together and add this mixture to the first four ingredients. Cover and chill for three hours.

Heat oven to 375 degrees. Roll the dough on a lightly floured cloth-covered board until it is approximately 1/4" thick. Cut into desired shapes and bake on lightly greased baking sheet for 7 or 8 minutes until lightly brown on the edges.

When the cookies are cool, frost them and tie them with ribbons. For example, you can tie ribbons around the bears' necks or the brims of the cowboy hats.

Tip: If you are free-forming the dough, it is not necessary to roll it out.

Cakes

If you decide to make the cake yourself, you have three options:

1. Bake the cake in a standard-sized rectangular, square, or round cake pan and decorate the top of the cake with theme-related decorations available at a party supply store.

2. Bake the cake in a pan that's already in the shape of your theme-related animal, character, or object. These cake pans are available at party supply stores, or through Wilton's Web site (see Resources). What I love about these pans is that they come with a sized picture that shows exactly what the finished cake should look like after it has been decorated.

3. Bake the cake in a rectangular pan and cut the pieces to form a theme-related shape. Tip: You can freeze a rectangular cake, use a toothpick to "draw" an outline of a theme-related shape; then, using a sharp knife, cut out the shape and frost. Many shapes can be drawn freehand, such as a dinosaur, cowboy boot, teddy bear, and so on.

Buttercream Frosting

Measure into a large mixing bowl:

☆ 1 1/4 cups shortening.

☆ 1 tsp. salt.

☆ 2 tsp. clear vanilla, lemon, or almond flavoring.

Beat at medium speed for three minutes.

Add all at once:

☆ 2 small boxes sifted confectioners' sugar.

☆ 9 Tbsp. milk or fruit juice.

Beat at medium speed until the consistency of whipped cream.

Decorate a Supermarket Cake

Character Bundt Cake

☆ One bundt cake.

☆ One can of frosting.

☆ One small plastic character or animal, appropriate to the party's theme.

Frost the cake. Insert the character into the hole in the center of the cake.

Barbie Doll Cake

☆ One angel food cake.

☆ One can of frosting.

☆ Food coloring.

☆ One Barbie doll.

☆ One glass jar or pint-sized milk carton.

Place the Barbie doll's legs into the jar or milk carton and insert in the center hole of the cake. Ice the cake with frosting to resemble a skirt. Fold the Barbie doll's real skirt over the top of the frosting "skirt."

A final tip

To add pizzazz to the top of any dessert before serving, add lighted sparklers or a lighted sugar cube dipped in lemon extract.

Chapter
74

Party Drinks

Here are popular party drinks served at children's parties:

- ★ Milk shakes.
- ★ Root beer floats.
- ★ Ice cream sodas.
- ★ Hot chocolate with marshmallows and whipped cream.
- ★ Hot cider served in mugs with cinnamon sticks.

Heavenly Party Punch

Place the following in a large punch bowl in this order:

- ★ Two quarts chilled fruit punch.
- ★ One quart raspberry sherbet.
- ★ Ice cold raspberry soda or ginger ale.

The sherbet will foam and bubble when the carbonated drink is poured over it, giving it a "heavenly" appearance.

Hawaiian Volcano Punch

(see Chapter 39).

Pumpkin Punch

(see Chapter 24).

Bug Punch

Any kind of fruit punch served in a punch bowl with ice cubes frozen with raisins inside.

Slurpies

Freeze three different fruit juices, such as grape, pineapple, and orange, in ice-cube trays. Place the ice cubes in a blender one flavor at a time and blend just until slushy. Layer the three flavors in tall, clear glasses.

Non-Alcoholic Smoothies

The ingredients in each of these recipes should be blended together to make one large smoothie:

Peanut Butter Smoothie

- ☆ 1 cup frozen vanilla yogurt.
- ☆ 1/2 cup apple juice.
- ☆ 1/2 cup peanut butter.
- ☆ 1/2 cup honey.

Strawberry Monkey

- ☆ 1 cup frozen strawberry yogurt.
- ☆ 1/2 cup fresh strawberries.
- ☆ 1 banana.
- ☆ 1 cup orange juice.

Berry Surprise

- ☆ 1 cup frozen vanilla yogurt.
- ☆ 1 cup raspberries.
- ☆ 1 cup blackberries.
- ☆ 1/2 cup apple juice.

Moonbeam

- ☆ 1/2 honeydew melon, peeled, seeded, and chopped.
- ☆ 1 apricot, pitted, and chopped.
- ☆ 1 cup ginger ale.
- ☆ 2 peaches, pitted and chopped.

Blend the fruits together until smooth. Add the ginger ale *very* slowly, and mix gently.

Polynesian Smoothie

- ☆ 1 banana.
- ☆ 6 oz. pineapple juice.
- ☆ 2 tsp. sugar.
- ☆ 1 cup frozen vanilla yogurt.

Shamrock Smoothie

- ☆ 1 cup frozen lime sherbet.
- ☆ 6 oz. pineapple juice.
- ☆ 1 cup lemon-lime soda.
- ☆ 1 drop green food coloring.

Cappuccino Smoothie

- ☆ 1 cup milk.
- ☆ 1/2 cup Cool Whip (frozen).
- ☆ 1 envelope instant cappuccino mix.
- ☆ Chocolate sprinkles

Blend milk and cappuccino mix well; then add Cool Whip. Top with more Cool Whip and chocolate sprinkles.

Shirley Temples

For each Shirley Temple, combine:

- ☆ 8 oz. cold ginger ale.
- ☆ 1 1/2 oz. bottled cherry juice.
- ☆ 1/2 cup crushed ice.
- ☆ 1 maraschino cherry.

Part

10

Stress-free Planning Sheets

Once you've selected your theme and you have an idea of what you'll do in the way of games, entertainment, and your party menu, all you need are a few easy, fill-in-the-blanks planning sheets. That's what you'll find in this section.

Make copies of the sheets and insert them in a lightweight three-ring binder. That way you'll have them handy as you plan your party. Just fill in the blanks and you'll have it made! You'll not only know what to do, when to do it, and how much everything will cost, but you'll have a complete shopping list all ready to go.

Chapter
___
75

Party Planner Countdown

Can be done weeks in advance

- ☐ Discuss party plans with your child or guest of honor.
- ☐ Enlist a co-host or volunteer(s) to help with the party plans.
- ☐ Choose a party theme.
- ☐ Choose a party site and place a deposit, if applicable.
- ☐ Compose the guest list with addresses and phone numbers.
- ☐ Buy or make the invitations.
- ☐ Buy stamps.
- ☐ Address the invitations.
- ☐ Plan the menu.
- ☐ Plan the games/activities/entertainment.
- ☐ Purchase supplies for decorations/favors/prizes.
- ☐ Arrange for any party props or decorations that need to be rented or borrowed.
- ☐ Buy paper goods (tablecloth, plates, cups, and napkins).
- ☐ _____
- ☐ _____
- ☐ _____

Two weeks before the party

- ☐ Mail or deliver the invitations.
- ☐ Begin assembling or making decorations/favors/prizes.
- ☐ Buy food items.
- ☐ Do advance food preparation.
- ☐ Order cake, deli foods, and specialty foods, if applicable.
- ☐ _____
- ☐ _____
- ☐ _____

One week before the party

- ☐ Make or buy name tags.
- ☐ Make or buy place cards, if applicable.
- ☐ Call your co-host or helpers to arrange a time to decorate and set up.
- ☐ Begin making decorations, favors, etc.
- ☐ Prepare music/cassette/CD player for the party.
- ☐ See if your camera is working correctly; be sure you have plenty of film.
- ☐ Place order with florist, if applicable.
- ☐ Decide what you and your child will wear to the party and have it ready for the big day.
- ☐ _____
- ☐ _____
- ☐ _____

A few days before the party

- ☐ Call guests who have not RSVP'd to see if they are coming.
- ☐ Once you know which guests are coming, begin filling out place cards and name tags, if applicable.
- ☐ Assemble any serving dishes, tableware, etc.
- ☐ Shop for perishable party food items.
- ☐ _____
- ☐ _____
- ☐ _____

One day before the party

- ☐ Meet with your helpers to do anything that can possibly be done in advance to avoid stress on the big day (decorate, make favors, set table, prepare food dishes, and so on).

☐ Clean house or arrange patio, pool chairs, etc. for party.

☐ Childproof your house—put away breakables and make sure medications, solvents, poisons, insect sprays, and so on are out of reach.

☐ Assemble game/craft supplies.

☐ Call to confirm time of pick-up or delivery from bakery, deli, or florist on the big day.

☐ _____

☐ _____

☐ _____

The big day

☐ Arrange to have one of your helpers pick up last-minute items, such as the cake, deli foods, rental chairs, helium balloons, and so on.

☐ Blow up balloons, if applicable.

☐ Last minute table setting.

☐ Last minute decorations, including exterior decorations, such as luminaries on front walkway or balloons tied to gate or entryway.

☐ Last-minute food preparations.

☐ Be dressed and ready for the party at least an hour in advance, just in case something unexpected happens (one of the guests needs a ride to the party at the last minute, the bakery forgets your order and you need to make an emergency run to the supermarket bakery, and the like).

☐ _____

☐ _____

☐ _____

Chapter

76

Fill-in-the-Blanks Party Planner

Guest of honor

_____

Names of co-hosts or helpers

_____Phone:_____

_____Phone:_____

Date, Time, and place of party

_____ From:_____ To: _____

Party Location:_____

Theme

_____ Page:_____

Wording for the invitations

_____

_____

_____

Guest list

Invitations mailed to the following on (date)_____

_____	Phone: _____	RSVP: ☐
_____	Phone: _____	RSVP: ☐
_____	Phone: _____	RSVP: ☐
_____	Phone: _____	RSVP: ☐
_____	Phone: _____	RSVP: ☐
_____	Phone: _____	RSVP: ☐
_____	Phone: _____	RSVP: ☐
_____	Phone: _____	RSVP: ☐
_____	Phone: _____	RSVP: ☐
_____	Phone: _____	RSVP: ☐
_____	Phone: _____	RSVP: ☐
_____	Phone: _____	RSVP: ☐
_____	Phone: _____	RSVP: ☐
_____	Phone: _____	RSVP: ☐
_____	Phone: _____	RSVP: ☐
_____	Phone: _____	RSVP: ☐
_____	Phone: _____	RSVP: ☐
_____	Phone: _____	RSVP: ☐
_____	Phone: _____	RSVP: ☐
_____	Phone: _____	RSVP: ☐

Decorations

_____

_____

Favors and prizes

_____

_____

Party menu

_____

_____

Games and activities

_____

_____

_____

_____

Entertainment

_____

_____

_____

_____

Notes

_____

_____

_____

_____

Chapter

77

Party Budget and Shopping List

		Amount
Invitations		
☐	Store-bought invitations	$_____
☐	Supplies to create your own invitations	$_____
☐	Envelopes	$_____
☐	Stamps	$_____

		Amount
Destination		
☐	Site rental fee	$_____
☐	Per/person fees	$_____
☐	Catering/serving/clean-up fees	$_____
☐	_____	$_____
☐	_____	$_____

		Amount
Decorations		
☐	Crepe paper	$_____
☐	Balloons	$_____
☐	Construction paper	$_____
☐	Streamers	$_____

Decorations (cont.)   Amount

- ☐ Poster board $_____
- ☐ Banners $_____
- ☐ Candles $_____
- ☐ Flowers $_____
- ☐ Strings of lights $_____
- ☐ Rental or borrowed decorations: $_____
- ☐ _____ $_____
- ☐ _____ $_____
- ☐ _____ $_____

- ☐ Novelty or theme-oriented decorations: $_____
- ☐ _____ $_____
- ☐ _____ $_____
- ☐ _____ $_____
- ☐ _____ $_____
- ☐ _____ $_____
- ☐ _____ $_____

Paper products   Amount

- ☐ Paper plates $_____
- ☐ Paper cups $_____
- ☐ Paper napkins $_____
- ☐ Plastic or paper tablecloth $_____
- ☐ Plastic tableware $_____
- ☐ Place cards $_____
- ☐ Name tags $_____
- ☐ Trash bags $_____
- ☐ _____ $_____
- ☐ _____ $_____

Party favors and prizes   Amount

- ☐ _____ $_____
- ☐ _____ $_____
- ☐ _____ $_____
- ☐ _____ $_____
- ☐ _____ $_____
- ☐ _____ $_____

Entertainment   Amount

☐ _____ $_____

☐ _____ $_____

☐ _____ $_____

Party Menu   Amount

☐ Bakery $_____

☐ Delicatessen/catering service $_____

☐ Supermarket purchases:

☐ _____ $_____

☐ _____ $_____

☐ _____ $_____

☐ _____ $_____

☐ _____ $_____

☐ _____ $_____

☐ _____ $_____

☐ _____ $_____

☐ _____ $_____

☐ _____ $_____

☐ _____ $_____

Miscellaneous   Amount

☐ Camera/film $_____

☐ Video tape $_____

☐ _____ $_____

☐ _____ $_____

☐ _____ $_____

☐ _____ $_____

Total cost of party: $_____

Afterword

I can't tell you how much fun I've had putting this book together for you! Some books are more fun to research and write than others, and this was definitely one of the highs of my writing career.

I hope you've found in this book just what you were looking for, and that every one of your parties is a huge success. As you have probably already figured out, this book is a keeper—one that will be handy to have on your shelf when the next party rolls around.

I will be updating this book from time to time, so I would love to hear from you. Please write me with your party experiences and ideas you've tried that can be included in the next edition of this book.

I can be reached through my publisher at the address shown here, or drop by and see me anytime at my Web site: www.dianewarnerbooks.com.

Diane Warner
c/o Career Press
P.O. Box 687
Franklin Lakes, NJ 07417

Resources

Books

Drucker, Malka. *The Family Treasury of Jewish Holidays*. Boston: Little, Brown, 1994.

Ehrlick, Amy. *The Story of Hanukkah*. New York: Penguin Books, 1989.

Ickis, Marguerite. *The Book of Religious Holidays and Celebrations*, New York: Dodd, Mead and Company, 1966.

Kimmelman, L. *Hanukkah Lights, Hanukkah Nights*, New York: Lothrop, Lee and Shepard Books, 1992.

Koch, Karl-Heinz. *Pencil and Paper Games*, New York: Sterling Publishing, 1991.

LeFanu, J. Sheridan. *Best Ghost Stories*, Mineola, N.Y.: Dover Publications, 1986.

Levie, Eleanor. *Halloween Fun*, New York: Berkley Publishing Group, 1993.

Maguire, Jack. *The Halloween Book*, New York, NY: Berkley Publishing Group, 1992.

Riddell, Mrs. J. H. *The Collected Ghost Stories of Mrs. J. H. Riddell*, Mineola, N.Y.: Dover Publications, 1974.

Salcedo, Michele. *Quinceañera; The Essential Guide to Planning the Perfect Sweet Fifteen Celebration,* New York: Henry Holt and Company, 1997.

Wiswell, Phil. *Great Party Games,* New York: Sterling Publications, 1988.

Party supplies

Advanced Graphics. (925) 432-2262. This company provides life-size standup cutouts of celebrities for your party. Pose your guests beside one of these and you'll have a great photo-op for your instant camera.

Andersons' Party Supplies. (800) 328-9640. Call to order their catalog, which features special theme decorations and favors.

Benco Party Favors. (800) 874-7970. Call for their catalog.

Birthday Express. (800) 424-7843. Call for their catalog.

Idea Art Catalog. (800) 433-2278. Great source of specialty papers suitable for laser printing.

Lighter Side Catalog. (941) 747-2356. Includes "Host Your Own Murder Mystery" party game.

Oriental Trading Company. (800) 228-2269. Call for their catalog which features party favors, decorations, name tags, invitations, place cards, and affordable gifts.

Sally Distributors. (800) 472-5597. Their catalogs feature colorful party decorations, favors, and costumes.

Sherman Party Theme Novelties Catalog. (800)645-6513, Ext. 3025. Their catalog features party favors, hats, and other theme novelty items, including karaoke party props.

Stump's Party Supplies and Decorations. (800)348-5084. This is a great source for theme party props and decorations.

U. S. Toy Company. (800)255-6124. Call for their catalog. It is filled with party supplies, favors, and such specialty items as carnival supplies.

Wilton Yearbook of Cake Decorating. (Woodridge, Il.: Wilton Enterprises, 2000.) If you're planning on baking and decorating a cake for your party, you'll find creative theme ideas in this book. It is available at all party supply stores.

Music

Sing Along Birthday Songs (recorded by Book Peddlers, Minnetonka, Minn., 1996) a musical tape with 19 favorite sing-along party and game songs for children's birthday parties, is available for less than $10 from Practical Parenting at (800) 255-3379.

Web Sites

Michael's stores—*www.michaels.com.* Craft instructions for your party.

Recipe encyclopedia—*www.epicurious.com.* Recipe suggestions.

Wilton Enterprises—*www.wilton.com.* Great ideas for cake decorating.

www.smarterliving.com/i.party—a Web site with ideas for "smarter living"

Index

Notes

Notes

Notes